BOOK 5

War

BY J.D. CRIST

I0694990

Copyright © 2025 by Pumpkin Head
Publishing

All rights reserved.

No portion of this book may be reproduced
or used in AI in any form without written
permission from the publisher or author,
except as permitted by U.S. copyright law.

Dedication

I am met with mixed emotions as Emily's story comes to a close. I have lived with this story for so long, and it has been a scary journey to share it with all of you. It makes me sad to have finished this story, but I couldn't be happier to know that so many of you have joined me on the journey. To my friends and family, I thank you for supporting me as I made every step along this road. Without your love and support, I would have never made it. To the fans, I can never express how grateful I am to every one of you. It is you who truly brought Emily and her story to life.

Trigger Warnings

This book contains several themes and topics that some people might be uncomfortable with. These include:

Death

Zombies

Murder

Child Abuse

Death

Child Death

If you are unable to continue, I understand. If you are, welcome to the world of The Dead Flash.

.

Chapter 1

Emily walked towards the school holding Hope and Steven's hands. They both insisted on staying close these past few weeks. While there had been no sign of any living outside the wall, the dead continued to come. The echoes of the groans and bodies hitting the wall could be heard throughout Sanctuary. She had to admit that the sound made her a little uneasy, but it also gave her comfort, knowing that no one could get near the wall.

"Maybe we shouldn't celebrate this year," Hope said softly as they walked.

"Shouldn't celebrate what?" Emily asked. "Your birthday?"

"Yeah," Hope nodded. "It doesn't seem right."

Emily stopped and knelt to look at her. She knew that Hope was having a hard time with everything that was going on. She had been protected inside the walls since the day she was born. Steven had an easier time, having lived on the move for so long.

"Is it because of the monsters?" Steven asked, looking at Hope.

"Yeah," Hope nodded. "The dead ones and living ones."

"You can't let them have that power over you," Emily said, looking at Hope. "They don't want us to be happy, to live."

"So that's what we have to do," Steven nodded.

"Will anyone even want to have a party?" Hope said with tears in her eyes.

"Are you kidding me?!" Emily said with a grin. "Julia has been bragging about how this will be your best cake! I have spent the past week helping people plan."

"Really?" Hope said as a smile crept across her face.

"I already got you a present," Steven grinned.

"I guess we can do it for them," Hope said, looking at them with a sheepish smile.

"And you," Emily said, letting go of their hands and tickling Hope.

"And me!" Hope squealed.

"That's better," Emily said as she stood and retook both of their hands. "Now, let us get you both to school before we get in trouble for being late."

"Are you picking us up today?" Steven asked as they reached the gate.

"I'm not sure," Emily smiled at him. "It will either be Uncle Joe or me. Is that okay?"

"Yeah," they both answered.

"Are you excited for me or Uncle Joe?" Emily asked, looking at them both, surprised.

"Love you," Hope said with a quick hug as she ran into the school.

"Love you," Steven echoed as he did the same.

"Love you guys too," Emily laughed as she waved and watched them go in.

Part of her hated having to drop them off. It meant that the time of smiles and the lighthearted conversation was over. Now she had to get back to work. She made her way to the town hall with Marley. As she walked, she saw that the sounds filling Sanctuary were affecting everyone. Usually, everything seemed light, and the faces of everyone she passed offered friendly smiles. But since the dead had arrived, everyone looked like they were at a funeral.

Emily walked into the town hall and made her way to her office. This would just be a quick stop today. She had done the reports the night before and just needed to file them away for today. She quickly slid each into the proper folder and turned to leave. Marley had already lain down and looked at her with heavy eyes.

"Not you too," Emily said as she sat on the couch.

Marley walked over and placed his head on her lap.

"It's just temporary," Emily assured him as she petted his head. "As soon as I figure out a plan, we will make them all go away."

Marley huffed, showing his discontent. Emily couldn't help but feel the same way. It had been weeks, and she still had no plan. They had walked Will and the others through Sanctuary, told them the rules, and each signed the ledger. Shawn insisted that they all be assigned to him, Sanctuary's private army. This meant that townspeople had to take way fewer shifts on the wall. No one seemed to mind, but no one seemed to entirely trust them either.

Emily tried her best to remember all the bikers' names, but still drew a blank most of the time. Usually, she was good with names, but they had never taken in a group of one hundred people at once. Thankfully, Shawn was with her most of the time and could help her. She avoided having to say their names directly when he wasn't.

Dillon was still staying on their couch, and Emily was in no hurry to push him into an apartment. He suffered from nightmares almost every night. Doc diagnosed him with PTSD from what he saw and did when with The General. Emily had tried to wake him from the nightmares the first time it happened. He swung at her and hit her hard before realizing where he was. Shawn was furious, but Emily assured him it was her fault. Dillon felt horrible and had offered to leave.

He only agreed to say after Emily, and the kids promised to stay out of the living room while he was sleeping. Now, only Shawn would try to wake him from his nightmares. He didn't talk much about what happened during his time at the compound, at least to Emily. But the few things that he did let slip were horrible. He kept up his usual defense of sarcasm and humor every time she tried to ask him about it. He was assigned as Shawn's assistant for a job, giving Shawn time to help him through what he had been through and keep an eye on him.

Veronica and Chad were still in prison cells. They moved them to separate cells, which gave Veronica another reason to scream. Chad had become his usual charming self. He no longer tried to be friendly and play with Emily's emotions. He was just as cruel and harsh as Veronica. Emily had talked with the council several times about what to do with them. They had agreed that they needed to keep them, just in case, until this war was over.

"War," Emily said to herself. "Who would have thought we would end up at war with The General?"

Marley huffed again and looked towards the door.

"You alright?" Shawn asked, leaning against the doorway.

"Just thinking," Emily said back as she looked at Marley.

"Care to share?" Shawn said, walking into the office and sitting down beside her.

"Nothing new," Emily admitted. "Just wanting this to be over with."

"I know," Shawn said, putting his arm around her. "We all do."

"Hope tried to cancel her birthday," Emily said, leaning into his chest.

"She can't do that," Shawn said, pulling her back and looking at her. "I told all the guys that she loved handmade gifts. Have you ever seen bikers try to use glue and glitter? They will be heartbroken."

"Steven and I talked her out of it," Emily laughed.

She couldn't help but picture all of the bikers sitting around craft tables trying to make things princess pretty.

"I was about to go pull her out of school," Shawn said, relaxing.

"I understand where she's coming from," Emily said, feeling sad again. "With everything going on, everyone looks so sad and worried. It just feels wrong to celebrate."

"Maybe the party is just what this place needs," Shawn replied after a moment. "Hope has always been the shining light that brings everyone together and makes them happy."

"I guess that's her superpower," Emily said.

Hope had once asked Emily if she was a superhero when she learned that the bites did not kill her. Hope called it her superpower.

"Then we finally have our theme this year," Shawn grinned. "Hope the superhero comes to the rescue."

"She'll love that," Emily smiled, pulling herself closer to him.

"The kids are going to be fine," Shawn said as he ran his hand across her hair.

"I just want them to have a normal life," Emily said, trying not to cry.

"They never will," Shawn replied.

Emily pulled back from him and could see that his face was serious.

"How can you say that?" Emily asked harsher than she meant to.

"It's the truth," Shawn said. "The days of Little League and family road trips are over."

"I know that," Emily said, confused.

"The day will come that they will have to handle things here," Shawn continued. "We can't shelter them from everything. We must ensure they know there are enough good moments to fight for, so they are ready."

Emily felt her anger drain away. She knew that he was right. They would have to face their war one day, no matter how much she wished they didn't.

"You're right," Emily finally said.

"Better write that down," Will laughed as he walked into the room. "I heard you only get five of those in a marriage."

"Sounds about right," Emily agreed. "And he used the first one, only being married two weeks."

"Man, you never use one in the honeymoon phase," Will teased as he walked closer.

"What would you know about it?" Shawn said teasingly.

"Three marriages," Will reminded him.

"Each ending after the five was used."

"I'll risk it," Shawn nodded after a moment. "It will be years before it happens again."

"He's not wrong," Emily agreed. "But I'm sure you came here for something other than marriage advice."

"Yeah, but this is more fun," Will grinned.

"Let us have it," Shawn said, motioning for Will to talk.

"Nothing big," Will said as he leaned against the desk. "Some of the guys reported seeing zombies in military uniforms. Just seemed like something you should know." "Some of them got bitten when we called them," Emily replied, not understanding.

"These wandered in from the east," Will continued. "They look, well, fresh."

"How many?" Shawn asked, leaning forward.

Emily joined him as she scooted forward herself. Maybe the camp had been attacked. Perhaps the dead had taken care of their problem for them.

"Maybe a handful," Will sighed. "Nothing to be excited about."

Emily sank back into the couch. She should have known it wouldn't be that easy.

"Could they tell how they died?" Shawn asked, not moving.

"Looks to be a shot to the chest," Will said, looking at Emily. "Definitely not accidental."

"We should ask Dillon," Shawn said, standing up.

"That's what I thought you might say," Will said, getting off the desk.

"Ask him what?" Emily asked, confused.

Dillon had been inside the wall. How would he know how the men were killed?

"Ask him how The General punishes people who displease him," Shawn said, looking down at her.

"You think he killed them?" Emily said, not trying to hide her disgust. "Why?"

"Could be anything," Dillon said as he walked into the room. "They could have been caught trying to leave, taken an extra ration, or crossed his path when he was in a bad mood."

Emily looked at Dillon as he spoke so casually. This must have been a common occurrence at the compound. Yet, his calmness about it made her uneasy.

"A shot through the heart was a standard punishment," Dillon continued.

"Why not the head?" Shawn asked, confused. "He had to know they were going to turn."

"He likes the dead," Dillon shrugged. "He used to give this speech, that it was an honor to be one of them. You could even be punished for putting one of them down."

Emily remembered calling in the dead while the bikers and the army were at the gate. Most of the soldiers, if grabbed, didn't try to fight it. They simply let the dead bite them.

"What if you're like Emily?" Shawn asked, pulling her back to the conversation. "And you can't become one of them?"

"That's why it's a shot to the heart," Dillon explained. "It will permanently kill anyone who can't return. He said it was part of the design."

"Part of the design?" Will asked, looking just as disturbed as Emily felt.

"I don't know," Dillon shrugged. "The world, maybe? You do know the guy's crazy, right?"

"I don't think even the crazies would claim him, son," Will said, turning back to Shawn. "He must think that Emily's kind is like an abomination or something."

"That's why he wants me dead," Emily spoke more to herself than to them. "Chad would have told him I was bitten and then found alive."

"Probably," Dillon nodded. "But you don't need to worry about that, beautiful."

Shawn glared at Dillon as he sat beside Emily and put his arm around her.

"You're safe," Shawn assured her.

Emily wanted his words to bring her comfort. She wanted her body to relax and feel safe inside these walls once more. She had always assumed he just wanted her dead because she led Sanctuary. But it was because she couldn't become a zombie.

"Wait," Emily said, having another thought. "One of the groups my family said they escaped from."

"One of the General's slaughters is more like it," Dillon scoffed, earning him another glare from Shawn.

"Yeah," Emily said, not noticing. "They said that the group worshiped the dead, and when it was time for you to move to the next level, they had a zombie chained up that you had to let bite you."

"What are you thinking?" Shawn looked at her, confused.

"Maybe Veronica had run out of stories to tell for the reason they had to run, so she told them what her dad believes," Emily said.

"That could be," Will said, looking at Shawn. "But what does that have to do with what's going on?"

"It means they might have told us more than they realize," Emily continued. "We just didn't know to pay attention."

Emily could see on Dillon and Will's faces that they thought she was going crazy. She turned to Shawn and hoped he understood what she was trying to say.

"We need to put together all the stories she told while they were here," Shawn offered after a few minutes. "See if we can find any similarities to the truth, and maybe we can find a hint as to their endgame or weakness.”

“Exactly!” Emily smiled as she looked back at Will and Dillon.

“Couldn’t hurt,” Will shrugged.

“You guys get started on that,” Emily said as she stood. She felt like she had a plan for the first time in weeks, giving her a sudden burst of energy.

“What are you going to do?” Shawn asked as he stood up beside her.

“I’m going to the source,” Emily grinned.

“That’s not a good idea,” Dillon said, looking worried.

“She’s locked up,” Emily insisted. “She can’t hurt me.”

“But you could say something you shouldn’t,” Dillon quickly responded. “Give her the upper hand.”

“In what?” Emily laughed. “Talking the cell door into opening for her?”

Dillon looked down at his shoes and looked hurt. Emily had not meant to hurt him with her words.

“I’ll be careful,” Emily insisted. “And if it makes you feel better, you can stand outside the door just in case.”

“I would feel better,” Shawn said, looking at Dillon. “You could stop her if anything starts to slip and be there if they get out somehow.”

"I can do that," Dillon nodded after a moment. "Yeah, that could work."

"Sounds like we all need to get to work then," Will said, walking towards the door. "What time is the party again?"

"Six," Emily replied. "Don't be late."

"So little time," Will said, being overdramatic. "What will I wear?"

Emily laughed with Shawn and Dillon as Will left.

"Do you want me to have Joe pick the kids up?" Shawn asked as he kissed Emily on the head and turned to leave.

"If you don't mind," Emily smiled at him.

"Just make sure you're not late," Shawn warned her as he left.

"You ready?" Emily said, turning to Dillon.

"Yes, ma'am," Dillon said in his military tone.

Emily hated it when he did that. She knew it was from years of living in the compound, but it made her uncomfortable.

"Emily," she reminded him. "At ease, soldier."

"Sorry," Dillon half-smiled. "Habit."

"I know," Emily smiled back.

Emily turned and walked to the security building with Dillon and Marley. She was surprised to see Sam and Alec playing their usual game of cards on the ground outside the door.

"Everything alright?" Emily asked as they neared them.

"So much more peaceful out here," Sam said, looking around.

The roar of the zombie crowd still echoed around them, bringing everyone else anything but a feeling of peace.

"Is she in a mood today?" Emily asked, looking at the door.

"I don't think you can call it a mood. It never ends," Alec said, looking up at her. "I think it's just called a personality."

"Does she ever get in storytelling moods when you guys are there?" Emily asked, looking back at them.

"When she's not screaming at us or telling us how we will die, yeah," Sam nodded. "Why do you ask?"

"We're having everyone write down all the stories she ever told them," Emily explained.

"Wanting to write a fiction book?" Sam asked, turning to look at her.

"Some of her stories are based on her dad," Emily explained. "We're trying to see if she let anything slip that we can use."

"Most of it seems like crap to me," Alec nodded. "But I'll write it down."

"Me too," Sam agreed. "Plus any new ones, she may tell."

"Does that mean we have to go back inside?" Alec said, pouting.

"Not yet," Emily laughed. "You guys keep playing for a bit. I'm actually headed in to listen to myself."

"You're a saint," Sam said, returning to their game.

"I don't know about that," Emily laughed as she reached for the door. "But feel free to pray for my sanity."

Sam nodded as Emily opened the door and walked inside with Dillon and Marley. Dillon shut the door once they were all in.

"Finally decide to feed us?!" Veronica's voice rang out.

Emily couldn't help but roll her eyes. She knew that they were being fed three times a day. This was just something else for Veronica to yell about.

"Lunch isn't for a few more hours," Emily responded after plastering on a smile.

"What are you doing here?" Chad snarled at her as she walked into view.

"Just came to talk," Emily smiled. "I miss you guys."

"Bullshit!" Chad yelled back. "Just get the fuck out!"

Veronica stood unusually silent as she appeared to be studying Emily. Emily walked casually to the table and pulled a chair closer to the cells. She said nothing as she sat down and smiled at both of them. Marley sat next to her, his body tense as he watched Chad and Veronica.

"So, how have you been?" Emily asked cheerfully.

"Fuck you!" Chad spat as he slammed against the door. "You've got us caged and living like animals. I think part of you is getting off on this!"

"God knows you never could do the trick," Emily said under her breath.

Veronica raised her eyebrow, and Emily knew that she had heard her. However, Veronica remained quiet and still didn't talk. Emily felt frustrated at how quiet she was being. Normally, Veronica would have been screaming by now, and Emily knew that she was playing her own game.

"What about you, Veronica?" Emily asked with a smile. "How have you been?"

"Fine," Veronica shrugged. "Though, if you plan on keeping us in here much longer, you could provide us with a few more comforts."

"Comforts are not something you should get used to," Emily said, shaking her head. "Though I may arrange for you two to have more toiletries. The smell in here is getting unbearable."

"Really!?" Veronica yelled, her cool demeanor disappearing and her vicious side taking over. "You are really going to talk shit about how we smell when you are the one keeping us locked in here?!"

"Just making conversation," Emily shrugged. "I honestly expected more from a woman who likes to sleep with married men." Veronica's face turned red as Emily looked at Chad.

"If you wanted a woman to look and smell like shit, you should have just told me," Emily smiled at him.

"You bitch!" Veronica yelled as she ran towards the door of her cell. "I will fucking kill you!"

"I'm scared," Emily said as she relaxed back in her chair. "The only person I know of that's more pathetic than the two of you is The General."

"You have no idea what you're talking about!" Veronica yelled as she slammed against the door.

"I don't," Emily said, raising her eyebrow this time. "I know plenty."

"The General always gets what he wants," Chad glared at her. "And what he wants is you dead."

"And he has a hard-on for zombies and punishes anyone who puts them down," Emily said, bored. "I really hoped you two had something new to tell me."

"He's a genius!" Veronica yelled. "You're nothing but a false prophet!"

"Prophet?!" Emily laughed. "So, now he thinks he's God?"

"You have no idea who he is," Veronica snarled.

"Maybe you should tell me?" Emily said casually. "Help me see why I should be scared and just surrender to him."

Chapter 2

Emily walked back out of the security building, no longer capable of intelligent thought. She had been listening to Veronica for hours, and her brain felt numb. According to how Veronica described The General, the man could walk on water if he chose. Emily knew that most of what she had just listened to was nothing but lies. All she had learned was that The General was more than a leader of an army. If what Veronica said was true, he was also the leader of a cult.

"That seemed like a waste of time," Dillon said as he shut the door behind her.

"Maybe," Emily sighed. "But maybe there was something in all that we can use." "She's just as crazy as The General," Dillon said as they began to walk with Marley.

"You should probably write down or tell someone everything you saw in the compound," Emily said, looking at him. "Do people there really believe half the crap she was saying?"

"Some," Dillon nodded. "Most."

"It may help us understand how to get him off his game," Emily sighed. "If you could write it down, we can try to figure something out."

"You don't want me writing anything," Dillon laughed.

"Why?" Emily asked, confused.

"My handwriting is awful," Dillon continued to laugh, looking at her.

"Oh," Emily smiled. "Maybe tell someone and have them write it down for you."

"Not sure who would want to sit and listen to all that," Dillon replied.

"Shawn would help," Emily offered. "Or I could do it."

"You?" Dillon said, looking at her. "I'm sure you have better things to do."

"You want to force me into listening to more of her stories, don't you?" Emily teased.

"That is the most extreme form of torture I've ever heard of," Dillon laughed. "I will do anything to save you from that."

"You really are a true gentleman," Emily grinned at him.

Emily looked around and could see that the party setup was nearly done. Despite the groans of the zombies, everything seemed to be almost perfect.

"When do you want to start?" Dillon asked as he stopped walking.

"Whenever you want," Emily replied. "I don't want you to do something you are not ready for."

"Do you think it will help with the nightmares?" Dillon asked sheepishly.

"It could," Emily said. "It wouldn't hurt to try."

"We can start tomorrow," Dillon nodded. "Just not at the house, though."

"We could use my office," Emily offered.

"That will work," Dillon agreed. "The kids don't need to hear this stuff."

"Let's not worry about this today," Emily smiled at him. "We have a party to focus on."

"Now that I'm here, it's really a party," Dillon cheered.

"Why don't you go see if they need help, and I'll go find the birthday girl?" Emily laughed, rolling her eyes.

"On it," Dillon nodded as he walked away.

Emily turned and made her way to the apartments. She couldn't help the happiness Dillon felt willing to talk to her. She thought for sure he would either decline or have Shawn help him. She knew he had been through a lot and hoped talking about it would help him. Emily and Marley made their way to Joe's apartment.

"You have to be cheating!" Joe's voice rang out inside the apartment.

"No," Steven laughed. "You're just really bad at this game."

"I'm getting hustled by kids," Joe said.

Emily laughed as she opened the door and walked in. Joe was sitting at the living room table with the kids. Emily laughed even harder to see that they were playing Candy Land.

"You know it's impossible to cheat at that game," Emily said to Joe.

"For normal people," Joe replied. "But I'm playing with a couple of genius kids."

Steven and Hope both laughed as they began to pick up the game.

"Next time we're playing poker," Joe said as he stood up.

"What's the buy-in?" Hope asked, smiling at him.

"How does she know what a buy-in is?" Joe said, looking at Emily.

"The security guys play," Emily laughed. "She may have picked up a few things."

"What game can I win?" Joe asked, flustered.

"Give it up, bro," Emily grinned.

"Beer pong!" Joe said, sounding almost serious.

"You're not getting my kids drunk," Emily laughed.

"Fine," Joe pouted. "But as soon as they're old enough…."

"You'll lose another game?" Steven smiled, putting the game back on the shelf.

Emily couldn't help but snort as she laughed hard. Joe grabbed Steven and began tickling him.

"Alright," Emily said as she saved Steven from Joe. "We should probably head down to the party."

"I'll be right there," Joe said as he walked back into the apartment. "Just gotta wrap the present."

Marley led them all out of the apartment.

"Are you sure everyone still wants to do this?" Hope asked as they walked down the stairs.

"Definitely," Emily nodded. "There was even talk of bikers using glitter to make your presents."

"What?" Steven laughed.

"Yup," Emily smiled. "Everyone is going all out."

"I can't wait for my birthday," Steven said as they walked outside. "Will I get a big party too?"

"Of course," Emily nodded.

Emily walked with them towards the house. The music was already playing, and she was grateful. It drowned out the moans and zombie sounds, even if it was just for one night. Hope and Steven ran off to play as soon as they saw the other children.

"She looks happy," Shawn said as he walked up and put his arms around her.

"Much better than this morning," Emily agreed.

"How did your afternoon go?" Shawn asked as he took her hand and led her to a table.

"Uneventful," Emily sighed. "She talked my ear off, and I feel dumber for listening."

"Any chance there was something useful?" Shawn asked as they sat down.

"Maybe," Emily replied.

"Dillon told me about him telling you everything he saw at the compound," Shawn said, taking her hand.

"He wants to start tomorrow," Emily nodded. "You think he's ready for that?"

"He needs to tell someone," Shawn said. "He tells me little bits but not much."

"Are you upset that he wants to tell me?" Emily asked.

"Not at all," Shawn said, shaking his head. "No offense, but he could tell Marley, and I would be thrilled. He just needs to get it all out."

"If only Marley could write," Emily sighed as she patted him.

"If only," Shawn agreed.

"No more tonight," Emily said, looking back at Shawn. "Tonight, there is no war, and we're just here to celebrate Hope's third birthday and another year safe inside the wall."

"It's hard to believe it's been three years," Shawn said, looking at Hope.

"I know," Emily agreed.

The party continued as usual. Everyone was gathered in front of Emily's house to take the yearly picture before the cake and presents. Hope sat at the table after, opening each gift with care and making sure to thank each person. Emily watched her proudly as it took her over an hour to get through them all. Most were books; her dream was to build a library, and others were small, handmade things. Hope adored each one of them.

Jose had built Hope another bookshelf for her room, and Derick made her a chest for the foot of her bed. Hope immediately began to fill the trunk with all the handmade gifts so they would stay safe. Emily couldn't help but admire how careful she was with each.

"My turn," Shawn said as he stepped forward and handed her a small box.

Hope eagerly opened the box and gasped at what was inside.

"What is it?" Emily asked, stepping forward.

"A locket," Hope said as she lifted the necklace out of the box and opened it. "With your and daddy's picture inside.

"This way, we will always be with you," Shawn smiled. "Even when we have to go outside the wall."

"I love it," Hope said as she ran towards Shawn and had him help her put it on.

"I guess it's my turn," Emily said as Hope turned the locket between her fingers.
"But for mine, we have to take a little walk." Hope ran towards her and took her hand. Everyone already knew what Emily was doing and waited as Shawn and she walked Hope towards the armory.

"My presents in here?" Hope asked as they walked in.

"Yes," Emily nodded as she walked to one of the gun lockers with Hope's name on it.

"A locker?" Hope asked, looking at her, confused.

"Open it," Emily said, motioning to the locker.

Hope slowly reached up and opened the locker. Inside was a small handgun and a box of ammo. Hope looked back at Emily, both excited and confused.

"You're only allowed to use it with Daddy or me," Emily said sternly. "And just for practice."

"Thank you, Mommy," Hope said, slamming the locker shut and wrapping her in a hug.

"You've done pretty well with the bed monsters," Emily laughed. "Just promise me you'll be careful."

"Yes, ma'am," Hope nodded. "Can Steven practice with us too?"

"Maybe," Shawn said as he walked in. "I might set up something for all the town kids to start learning."

"They all want to," Hope nodded.

"But only if they keep up with their school work and chores," Emily added.

"Of course," Hope agreed. "Thank you."

"You're welcome," Emily laughed. "You'd better get back to your party."

"Oh yeah," Hope said as she ran back out the door.

"I never thought you'd go through with it," Shawn said as he took her hand and led her outside.

"She really wants to learn, and looking at her, she looks old enough to learn," Emily said, still trying to convince herself that this was a good idea. "Plus, they'll never have a normal life."

"That's right," Shawn said as he kissed her hair. "But normal was boring anyway.

The rest of the party went smoothly, and Emily ended up with the town's kids at her house for a sleepover. She set them up with snacks and then left them to their own devices.

"I think we did it," Emily smiled as she closed the bedroom door.

"Did what?" Shawn asked, sitting up in the bed.

"We managed to do one thing that The General could not ruin," Emily answered, climbing into bed beside him.

"It's all because of you," Shawn said, pulling her close.

"It's because of all of us," Emily replied. "I couldn't do anything without everyone here."

"Whatever you say," Shawn said as he closed his eyes.

Emily woke early the following day to prepare food for the army of kids before they woke. They hadn't made it long, and she knew they would be up soon. She had finished making the plates as they began to pile into the kitchen. Emily only caught a glimpse of Shawn getting his morning coffee and another as he blew her a kiss, heading out the door. It wasn't long after he left that the parents started arriving, and soon, the house was quiet again.

"Did you have a good birthday?" Emily asked Hope as she was grabbing one of her new books.

"The best," Hope smiled.

"I'm glad," Emily replied as she sat on the couch. "You guys will go to Grandma's for a while today."

"Are you working?" Hope asked, confused.

"Not really," Emily answered. "Uncle Dillon and I have some things to do."

"Where is Uncle Dillon?" Hope asked, looking around.

"He stayed with Uncle Joe last night," Emily said. "He didn't want to scare your friends if he had a nightmare."

"I wish those would go away," Hope said with concern.

"We're going to try something today to see if it might help," Emily assured her.

"Then to Grandma's, we go," Hope chirped, walking towards the door with her book.

"Aren't you forgetting something?" Emily smiled at her.

"Steven!" Hope said as she took off towards the stairs with Marley.

Emily waited by the front door for the three of them to return.

"Mommy almost forgot you," Hope said as she walked down the stairs. "But I remembered."

"Really?" Emily said, looking at her with one eyebrow raised.

"Just kidding," Hope laughed as she ran out the door.

"Sisters," Steven said, rolling his eyes before he took off after her.

Emily followed them both to Christine's house and waved goodbye as they went inside. She then turned with Marley and walked towards the Town Hall. She was surprised to see Dillon waiting for her outside the door.

"You ready to get started?" Dillon asked, opening the door.

"I am if you are," Emily said as she walked in.

Dillon didn't answer as he followed her and Marley inside. Emily led him to the office with Marley. Dillon walked straight to the couch and sat down.

"So, how do we do this?" Dillon asked, looking at her.

"I got this recorder," Emily said, setting an old tape recorder on the desk. "If it's okay with you, I could record what you say. That way, we can just talk."

"That'll work," Dillon nodded. "As long as I don't have to lie down."

"No," Emily laughed. "I'm not a therapist."

"Good," Dillion smiled. "Let's get this started then."

"Only if you're ready," Emily insisted. "We don't have to do this today."

"I need to," Dillon said flatly. "I lived it, and I can't separate what's normal and not anymore. Maybe you guys can find something that can help."

"Alright," Emily said as she turned on the recorder.

"Where do you want me to start?" Dillon asked.

"The flash," Emily suggested. "The very beginning."

"I was on my way to the clubhouse," Dillon started. "My mom had a "client" over, and I had to get out of there. I didn't make it far before the sky lit up."

"Did you make it to the clubhouse?" Emily asked.

"No," Dillon said, shaking his head. "Panic started, and I headed back up to the apartment."

Emily could see that Dillon was struggling to continue, and she didn't want to push. She waited quietly while he worked through his thoughts.

"By the time I got up there," Dillon said after a deep breath. "My mom was gone."

"She left?" Emily asked.

"No," Dillon said, shaking his head. "She was dead and eating the guy she brought home."

Emily sat in shock, unable to say anything.

"She looked at me as I walked in. Her eyes were different," Dillon continued. "She slowly got up off the floor and started walking towards me. I remember crying as I held her back, and she kept trying to bite me." "I can't imagine," Emily said.

"She backed me into the kitchen," Dillon continued. "With my free hand, I grabbed a knife off the counter. I apologized to her, and I…."

"Put her to rest," Emily offered as she watched him struggle.

"That's one way to put it," Dillon said, tears trying to build in his eyes.

"You were fourteen," Emily said, unable to imagine what he was feeling.

"Yeah," Dillon nodded. "I took out from there like the place was on fire. I ran to the clubhouse, but everyone was gone by the time I got there. Some of the guys were dead. Others were dead but walking around."

"Oh, my God." Emily felt the words escape before she could stop them.

"I just stood there like an idiot," Dillon said, visibly angry with himself. "The dead ones were moving close, and out of nowhere, someone grabbed my jacket and pulled me into a truck."

"Who was it?" Emily asked.

"The General," Dillon answered with a snarl. "He asked me what I was doing there and if there were any survivors. I told him I went there to look for my brother, Shawn, but found the place like that."

"Did he seem interested in Shawn right away?" Emily asked.

"Oh yeah," Dillon nodded. "He vowed right there that he would find him. I didn't think anything of it because I wanted to be with my brother."

"Of course," Emily tried to comfort him.

"He kept me close," Dillon continued, the tears in his eyes now gone and replaced with anger. "We went to the compound the next day. It was already set up. He said he had been planning for the worst."

"And the best he could come up with was that compound?" Emily couldn't help but feel disappointed. Robert planned for the worst, too, and built Sanctuary.

"He said he used to have a better place," Dillon replied. "A top-of-the-line facility, he called it. But some traitor blew the crap out of it, killing a bunch of his men." "Really?" Emily said, surprised.

"That was the story," Dillon shrugged. "Probably a bunch of crap."

"You're probably right," Emily nodded.

"I didn't leave that compound for years," Dillon said. "And neither did he. He kept me close, and I watched everything he did like he was grooming me or something."

"Or protecting his leverage for when he found Shawn," Emily offered.

"That seems more likely," Dillon said, looking at her for the first time. "You know, this is harder than I thought."

"We can stop for today," Emily smiled. "There's no rush."

"Yeah," Dillon nodded. "Maybe we can do more tomorrow."

"Whenever you're ready," Emily said as she turned off the tape recorder and put it away in her desk.

"So," Dillon grinned at her, "Who's story is better so far?"

"What do you mean?" Emily asked, looking back at him.

"Mine or Veronica's?" Dillon grinned.

Emily could tell that his defenses were back up.

"Yours, of course," Emily laughed. "Thank you for saving me from her today."

"My pleasure," Dillon said as he stood up and bowed to her.

Emily laughed as she walked out of the office with him. He was back to using humor and sarcasm, but she wasn't going to say anything about it. This was probably the first time he talked about the day of the flash with anyone, and she had to let him work through it.

Emily waited a few minutes and took out a notebook to write down what Dillon had told her. It was nice to have the recording, but maybe writing it down would help her. She turned on the recorder and listened to Dillon's words once more. Pausing every few moments and writing down what was said.

Emily pressed pause on the recorder and wiped the tears from her eyes. She could hear his pain about having to put down his mother. She knew from what Shawn had said that she was not the best person, but Dillon still loved her. Marley came up and nudged her. She ran her hand over his soft fur and felt herself relax. After a few moments, she pressed play and finished writing the rest of what Dillon had said.

Emily turned off the recorder the last time and looked back over the words.

"A top-of-the-line facility, he called it. But some traitor blew the crap out of it, killing a bunch of his men."

Something about that line stood out to Emily. She sat staring at the words, rewinding the recorder, and listening to them, trying to figure it out. Finally, she decided to take a break and come back to it. Perhaps as Dillon continued to talk, it would make more sense to her.

Chapter 3

Dillon was still not ready to continue the next day, and Emily did not push. She knew she was asking a lot of him, and pushing him could cause him to break. She instead focused on helping Shawn set up the weapons training class for the kids. She hadn't expected so many of the parents to want their kids trained as well. The threat of the war seemed to have them all on edge, and no one wanted their kids to be defenseless.

They worked on the curriculum, having regular council meetings to discuss their plan to ensure everyone was comfortable. The goal was to start with the anatomy of a zombie, then hand-to-hand, and last, firearms. Emily knew Hope was anxious to learn how to use the pistol, but she accepted that she needed to learn things in a particular order.

"She's doing quite well," Shawn said as they had lunch. "Especially learning how to take down someone bigger than her." "That's good," Emily sighed.

She was struggling with Hope learning how to fight. She still felt like she should be able to protect her daughter from everything.

"You should come out and watch them today," Shawn said, looking at her knowingly.

"I've got work to do," Emily replied quickly.

She had agreed to let the kids train, but wasn't ready to see them doing it.

"She wants you to come," Shawn said, taking her hand.

Emily looked up at him with pain in his eyes. She could tell that Hope had asked him to get her to come.

"I can try to stop by for a bit," Emily conceded.

"Will you actually try, or will you find another excuse?" Shawn asked her.

"I'll stop by," Emily assured him.

This wasn't the first time she had promised to try. The other times, she hid in her office and didn't come out until the training was over. She wanted to do the same thing today, but knew she couldn't. Hope had given up asking her directly and was now sending Shawn.

"I'll tell her," Shawn said, finishing his lunch.

With that, Shawn cleaned up their lunch and headed back out. Emily stood from her chair and walked over to the window. She picked up the walkie she had set in the sunlight to charge. She had been spending a lot of time here and was afraid it would die. She clipped the walkie back on her waist and sat back down. She reached into her desk drawer and pulled out the tape of Dillon again. She placed the recorder on the desk and pressed play.

Emily was listening to the story again when someone entered through the doorway.

She glanced up to see Dillon standing there watching her.

"Hey," Emily said as she pressed stop on the recorder.

"You got a fresh tape?" Dillon asked, walking into the room.

"Uh, yeah," Emily said awkwardly. "I'm ready when you are."

"Probably should give you something new to listen to," Dillon smiled as he sat down on the couch.

Emily nodded as she removed the tape and put in a new one.

"You ready?" Emily asked him.

Dillon nodded yes, and Emily pressed the record button on the tape recorder.

"Last time you were saying that The General kept you close," Emily prompted Dillon to begin.

"Yeah," Dillon nodded. "My tent was next to his. I had to eat every meal with him. Now that I think about it, it was like we were married."

Emily could sense immediately that his defenses were still up as he began to laugh. Again, she knew not to push and waited patiently for him to continue.

"He did have me trained, though, "Dillon continued. "I knew how to fight, but this was different. I really sucked at it at first. I didn't want to train. I just wanted to find Shawn and get out of there. But as time went on, I began to take to it."

"What changed?" Emily asked.

"I gave up," Dillon sighed. "I knew the chance of my finding Shawn was next to nothing. That place was going to be where I was stuck. I could either get really good or end up with a bullet in my heart."

"So, you got really good," Emily nodded at him.

"Yeah," Dillon nodded. "And I began to get some work around the compound."

"He let you do things without him," Emily spoke.

"Yes," Dillon agreed. "But it was only stuff for him and the cause."

"Like what?" Emily asked, instantly regretting her question as Dillon's face dropped.

"I did it to survive," Dillon began defending himself. "I didn't know…." "I'm not judging you," Emily interrupted.
"You were just a kid in an impossible situation. You did what you had to."

"The General wanted the dead," Dillon said forcefully. "Killing one meant you had to take its place. If you were bitten and didn't turn, he burned you alive. The dead were everything to him."

"Did he ever say why?" Emily asked, trying to ignore The General's desire to burn her alive.

"People were sheep," Dillon continued. "The dead were pure. No alliances, just survival and all working together for the same goal."

"Since when is eating people a goal?" Emily said disgustedly.

Dillon stayed silent and shrugged.

"Is that what *religion* was based on?" Emily asked next.

"Probably," Dylan nodded. "I never bought into that, though. I just played my part in surviving."

"What kind of stuff did he have you do?" Emily asked.

"I became his enforcer," Dillon said, looking at the ground. "I killed people, however he judged."

"He made you shoot them," Emily said with pain in her heart.

"Or burn them," Dillon said, looking at her.

"Did he find a lot of people who were like me?" Emily asked.

"One hundred and twenty-six turned with a bullet to the heart, and forty-eight were burned alive," Dillon said with little emotion, not meeting her gaze.

"In total, or the ones he had you kill?" Emily asked, shocked by his answer.

"Those were my kills," Dillon said, still not looking at her.

"It's not your fault," Emily said, trying to comfort him.

"I pulled the trigger," Dillon said, standing up. "I lit the fucking match. I'm just as much a monster as that son of a bitch!"

"Would you burn me?" Emily asked as she stood and walked closer to him.

"Of course not," Dillon said with pain as he looked at her.

"Would you shoot anyone here?" Emily asked.

Dillon didn't reply and just looked at her with cold eyes.

"Other than Veronica and Chad," Emily quickly added.

"No," Dillon said, shaking his head.

"You're not a monster," Emily assured him. "You were a kid that was being used by a monster."

"I still see their faces," Dillon said as he turned towards her with tears in his eyes. "Every single one."

"That just proves my point," Emily said softly. "A monster doesn't care and wouldn't remember."

She suddenly understood what Dillon's night terrors were about. He was reliving each time The General made him kill. Dillon had been forced to kill almost two hundred people to defend himself and further the General's cause.

"I helped when I could," Dillon spoke again as he sat back down.

"How?" Emily asked, joining him.

"The scientists couldn't do what he wanted. They were trying to figure out the work of the one that got away," Dillon said. "He would starve them to try to make them work harder, but I would sneak them food and didn't beat them as he asked."

Emily felt her blood run cold as he spoke. Suddenly, everything seemed to fall into place, and she thought of Robert.

"Who got away?" Emily asked slowly, trying to hide the fear in her voice.

"Robert," Dillon said after a moment. "Robert Devow."

"Shit," Emily said as she walked over to the bookshelf.

"What is it?" Dillon asked, confused.

"Robert Devow built this place," Emily said, pulling out all of Robert's journals and stacking them on the desk. "He thought it was a military project to save endangered species or something being done by the government."

"The General," Dillon said, walking over and picking up one of the journals.

"He said that the man in charge called himself The General, but I never put it together," Emily said, frustrated with herself. "The General killed the other scientists. Who did he get to work on the research?" "I don't think they joined up willingly," Dillon said, flipping through one of the journals.

"Do you know what he has them working on?" Emily asked, looking back at him.

"A fix," Dillon said flatly. "For the mistakes with the original virus."

"Mistakes?" Emily said, confused.

"For people like you," Dillon said, closing the book and setting it back down.

"Robert designed the rejuvenation part," Emily said more to herself than to him. "Without changing that formula, he can't release another flash."

"You think he wants to do another flash?" Dillon said with anger in his eyes. "That could turn everyone."

"He didn't get time to perfect it before Robert escaped," Emily continued. "I'm sure he wants to make it, so he, his precious daughter, and a few others survive."

"But without Robert, he can't," Dillon said, turning away from the books. "So, he can't get what he wants unless he finds Robert."

"He's here," Emily said, thinking of the sign-out front with Roberts's name on it as the designer.

"Where?" Dillon said with his voice on edge.

"The cemetery," Emily said flatly. "He was the first one buried in it when it was just Marley and me here."

"You don't understand," Dillon said, getting agitated. "He hunted for Robert more than anyone else. He will do anything to find him."

"Maybe this will help," Emily tried to calm him. "Once he knows Robert's dead, he will have to give up his mission."

"No," Dillon said flatly, shaking his head. "He won't believe you and will burn this place to the ground looking for him."

"He can't get past the wall," Emily said, dismissing his worry.

"He doesn't have to," Dillon said, frustrated. "It's not like you can keep things from coming over."

"Over?" Emily said with fear in her voice.

Even though things technically could come over the wall, she had never thought anyone would have the capability of doing it. Most people were lucky to find the basics of survival today, but who knows what the General had access to? She looked back at Dillon and realized that he knew.

"Has he taken over a place like this before?" Emily asked slowly.

"Not exactly," Dillon admitted. "But there were a few places with walls he couldn't easily get into.""But he got in," Emily said, feeling the color drain from her face.

"He got them to come out," Dillon corrected her. "Honestly, most gave up after just a few days, but some...."

"Go on," Emily heard herself plead.

"It doesn't matter," Dillon said, plastering a smile on his face. "He's never come up against anyone like you or this place."

"Damn straight," Shawn said, walking in.

Emily glared at him, and he took a few steps back.

"What's going on?" Shawn asked, realizing he was missing something.

"The General," Emily said, motioning to the journals," He's the same one that started all of this."

"Shit," Shawn said, looking between her and Dillon.

"He wants to do it again," Emily continued, looking at Dillon.

"But he can't," Dillon said casually. "You said it yourself. Robert is dead."

"And you said he has ways of fighting over the wall," Emily felt her anger boil. "What has he done to the ones before? The ones that didn't surrender?"

"It doesn't matter, "Dillon repeated.

Almost as if he could sense that Emily was about to lose her temper, Shawn walked over and put his hands on her shoulders.

"He's right," Shawn said softly. "I thought he might try and have put precautions in place."

"What if it's not enough?" Emily said with tears in her eyes. "What if there is more we could do?"

"Short of putting on a roof, which we can't," Shawn smiled. "We are as prepared as we can be."

"I just don't know why he won't tell me," Emily said, looking back at Dillon.

"Hope told me what you said about her birthday," Dillon said, stepping forward. "About, we have to keep living despite him."

"What does that have to do with anything?" Emily asked, confused.

"I could tell you everything, and then you would spend every moment trying to find a way to counter it," Dillon continued.

Emily looked at him, confused.

"You would stop living, and he would win," Dillon finished.

"He's right," Shawn said, pulling her face towards him. "You just have to trust that we have done everything we can and will make it through this just like we have everything else."

"I'm scared," Emily admitted as the tears began to flow freely.

"So am I," Shawn said as he pulled her close.

Emily let his big arms surround her as she settled her face into his chest.

"I am, too," Dillon said softly.

Emily pulled away from Shawn and looked at him. He was no longer trying to act calm and collected and look vulnerable. She pulled herself away from Shawn and walked over to Dillon.

"What do you say we go live?" Emily smiled at him as she dried away her tears.

"There is a class of kids out there eager to show off their skills," Shawn offered, walking towards them.

"Let's do it," Dillon nodded.

Shawn turned and began to lead them out of the office. Emily grabbed Dillon's arm and stopped him once Shawn was far away.

"I'm sorry," Emily said as he turned towards her.

"Don't be," Dillon assured her. "If I thought it would help, I would tell you. I promise."

"I know," Emily nodded. "I trust you."

"Come here, sis," Dillon smiled as he hugged her.

Emily laughed as she hugged Dillon and then followed him outside. The kids were lined up on the main street, listening to Shawn as he gave them directions.

"Let's work hand in hand today," Shawn said to them with a smile. "Because the most important thing we are learning is…."

"To defend ourselves," the kids all replied in unison.

Emily couldn't help but smile as she sat down on the steps and watched.

"Exactly," Shawn nodded. "I know you are all having fun with the knife training, and some of you can't wait for the firearms training to begin."

Emily noticed that Shawn looked directly at Hope as he said the last part.

"But, self-defense is the most important part," Shawn continued. "We are going to try something different today."

Emily watched as Shawn motioned toward Will, and several bikers walked forward.

"These guys have put me on my butt more times than I can count," Shawn said to the children. "Let's see if you have been paying attention."

Shawn nodded, and the bikers each walked toward the kids. She watched as Will walked towards Hope, and Jerry walked towards Steven. They looked small compared to the grown men, but neither showed any fear.

"They will attempt to grab you and take you away," Shawn explained. "Their goal is to get you to the gate. Your goal is to stop them and get away. Remember to work together when you can."

With that, Shawn stepped back and stood next to where Emily and Dillon were sitting.

"Can they handle this?" Emily said, looking up at him.

"Just watch," Shawn assured her with a smile.

Emily turned her attention back to the kids. They had been working hard for the past month, but honestly, she had no idea what they could do. She watched as Will lunged at Hope, and Hope dropped to the ground and crawled between his legs.

"It's not all about strength," Shawn smiled as a look of pride spread across his face. Once Hope was free, she ran towards Jerry, who was backing Steven up slowly. Steven looked terrified as his eyes darted from side to side. Emily had to fight everything inside her that screamed to help him. Suddenly, the look of fear on Steven's face was replaced with a smile. Emily felt a wave of confusion wash over her as she saw the scene unfold. Hope reached Jerry without anyone seeing her and kicked him as hard as she could. Jerry's eyes began to water as he dropped to the ground. Hope ran straight to Steven and took his hand. They took off to help the other children.

"That was a bit…rough," Emily finally spoke, looking at Shawn.

"But effective as hell," Dillon laughed.

"I taught them to defend themselves," Shawn said. "In a fight, there is a winner and a loser. Why should kids fight fair when it's grown-ass adults attacking them?"

"Were the guys at least warned first?" Emily laughed as Jerry began to pick himself up from the ground.

"Maybe," Shawn grinned.

Emily watched as the kids worked together to fight off the bikers. The bikers were struggling to gain ground, but Will finally scooped up Bobby and began to run for the gate.

"Let me go!" Bobby yelled as he kicked and fought against Will.

"Got ya," Will smiled as he continued to run.

Emily looked back at the other kids and saw they didn't realize Bobby was missing. They were slowly working their way into the clinic and fighting to get the door closed. Emily looked back just as Will reached the gate with Bobby.

"That's it!" Shawn yelled, causing the commotion to stop.

"But the doors are not closed," Hope said, walking forward, confused.

"But Bobby is gone," he said to Hope while pointing at the gate.

"Shoot!" Hope said, looking at Bobby and Will.

Will had placed Bobby back on the ground, and the two of them were now laughing.

"What did we do wrong?" Hope asked as she walked towards Shawn with the other kids.

"You tell me?" Shawn said, looking at all of them. "Who's Bobby's buddy?"

"I never picked one," Bobby said, running up to join them. "I thought I would be fine on my own."

"There's your problem," Shawn said, looking at him sternly. "If you are alone, there is no one to help you when you get into trouble."

"Yes, sir," Bobby said, looking upset with himself.

"Who else doesn't have a buddy?" Shawn asked, looking at the kids.

Emily quickly counted them and realized that there was an uneven number.

"Everyone has a buddy?" Shawn said, looking at them all as they nodded. "Then what do we do?"

"He'll be with us," Hope said, stepping forward.

"Is that a good idea?" Shawn asked, looking at her. "It means that you have to watch out for two people."

"It also means two people are watching my back," Hope smiled at him.

"Alright," Shawn nodded. "Why don't you all break off into groups and practice more? Anyone who thinks they need medical attention can see Doc."

"I'm good," Jerry said as he walked slowly towards the apartments.

Emily watched as some others praised the kids and rubbed the fresh bruises that the kids had given them.

"What do you think?" Shawn said, walking back towards Emily.

"The General better watch out," Emily laughed.

Chapter 4

Emily tried to focus the next few weeks more on her family than on The General. She tried her best to remember that she still had to live. As time went on without sighting their enemy, she couldn't help but be hopeful that maybe he had given up. She had informed the council that the General was the same in Robert's journals as everything Dillon had told her.

Dillon's night terrors had only worsened since he told her the truth. Emily wished she could find a way to help him through it.

"I have an idea," Jose said, walking up beside her and making her jump.

"About how to give me a heart attack?" Emily said, placing her hand on her chest.

"No," Jose said, looking around. "About how to help Dillon."

"What?" Emily asked as she looked at him with curiosity.

"He remembers everything about them, right? He remembers their names?" Jose asked, looking around to make sure no one was listening.

"Yeah," Emily nodded. "It's like they haunt him in his dreams."

"Maybe they continue to haunt him because he's the only one left who knew that they existed, who remembers them," Jose continued.

"Maybe," Emily said, still confused.

"A memorial," Jose continued. "We could build a memorial for them, with all the information he can remember. Let him know that they will always be remembered, like Robert."

"That's an excellent idea," Emily said with a smile. "I'll talk to him about it tonight." "If he's willing, just send him to me," Jose smiled. "I'll make sure everything is taken care of."

Emily nodded as Jose took off towards the construction area. Emily went to the bakery, where Julia was waiting to have lunch with her. Emily made it a point not to be alone as much as possible. Being alone made it easy for her to slip back into her obsession.

"Right on time," Julia smiled as she walked in.

"No one else eating today?" Emily said, looking around at the empty tables.

"People have been spending more time at home lately," Julia shrugged as she set two plates on the table.

"I'm sure they'll be back," Emily said as she turned her attention to her lunch.

"Just a lot going on," Julia smiled. "It even took you a while to want to get back to normal."

"Normal," Emily grinned. "I'm anything but normal."

"Well, normal for you," Julia laughed.

"How's Bobby doing?" Emily asked as she continued to eat.

"Good," Julia nodded. "He's not scared anymore."

"That's good," Emily replied.

"How's Dillon?" Julia asked, taking a bite of her sandwich.

"Same," Emily sighed. "But Jose had an idea that might help."

"Really?" Julia asked, looking at her.

"Yeah," Emily nodded. "I'm going to talk to Dillon about building a memorial for the people he was forced to…you know."

"It's worth a try," Julia nodded. "I'm sure we could get the whole town to help dedicate something tasteful."

They continued their small talk as they each ate. Julia never forced Emily to talk but always had something kind to say when she did. Lunch was over quickly, and Julia returned to work after clearing the plates. Emily walked back onto the main street and was surprised to find Marley sitting outside waiting for her.

"Aren't you supposed to be with Hope?" Emily smiled as she petted his head.

Marley wagged his tail in excitement as she spoke. He had been extra clingy since The General had made his presence known.

"Hope sent him," Will smiled as he walked towards her. "She wants to learn to defend herself more, and Marley kept trying to defend her."

Marley wagged his tail as if happy to hear Will brag about his accomplishments.

"You can defend me for a while then," Emily said as she scratched behind his ear.

"Alec actually sent me," Will said, causing her to look back at him. "The prisoners have been demanding to speak with you. I'm pretty sure if you don't talk to them soon, he may just kill them."

"That bad?" Emily asked, looking towards the security building.

"Pretty bad," Will nodded. "You want me to go with you?"

"I think I'm okay," Emily said, looking down at Marley.

Will nodded as Emily walked towards the security building with Marley. As she approached, she could hear familiar screams from Veronica inside. Emily pushed the door open and saw Alec at the table with his head in his hands. He looked up at her, relieved as she walked in.

"You can't just keep us here forever!" Veronica shrieked from her cell.

"Have no intentions of it," Emily smiled at Alec. "Why don't you take a break? I got this."

"You sure?" Alec asked as he jumped up and made his way toward the door.

"I'm sure," Emily laughed.

"It's about time you came back!" Veronica yelled at her.

"Did you miss me?" Emily smiled as she pulled a chair closer.

"Where's our son?" Chad asked, standing up in his cell.

"My son," Emily replied with a glare. "He is at training with his father." "You bitch!" Veronica spat at her.

"Do you have anything new to say or what?" Emily sighed.

She was not in the mood to hear the two of them scream the same things repeatedly.

"I can't wait until he kills you," Veronica glared at her.

"I'll take that as a no," Emily sighed as she stood up and put the chair away.

Emily made her way to the door. She planned on waiting outside for Alec to return from his break.

"You should turn on your damn phone!" Veronica yelled at her, causing her to stop midstep.

She knew the phone Veronica was talking about. Shawn had locked it up in the armory once they had gotten back and never turned it on. She turned and slowly looked at Veronica. Emily grabbed the keys from the desk and quickly made her way to Veronica's cell. She quickly unlocked the door and grabbed Veronica's hair. Veronica screamed as Emily pulled her out of the cell and slammed her against the wall.

"How do you know I'm not answering the phone?!" Emily snarled, inches from her face.

"Just a guess," Veronica cried in pain.

Emily knew that she was lying. Veronica didn't guess. She knew. She always had to have a plan for everything she did. Emily pushed Veronica hard to the ground and turned to walk into the cell.

"Stop it!" Veronica yelled as she tried to get up from the floor.

Emily heard a low growl and knew that Marley was keeping her still. Emily quickly set to work, going through the few things in the cell. She sighed as she came up with nothing. Emily looked at Chad's cell and realized how quiet he had been during everything. He was pushed against the opposite wall, staring at the floor.

"Give it to me," Emily snarled at him.

"I don't know what you're talking about," Chad said, not looking at her.

"Now," Emily said, moving closer to the bars.

She knew that deep down, Chad was a coward, and she was in no mood to play games. Chad stepped forward and handed her a phone.

Emily glared at the phone as she took it from him.

"How did you get this?" Emily asked as she glared at him.

"I don't know," Chad said, backing away from her.

"How did you get this?!" Emily yelled as she reached through the bars and slammed his face into them.

"I don't know," Chad cried out. "She had it when I woke up a few weeks ago."

Emily released Chad and turned back to Veronica. She was still seated on the floor, Marley baring his teeth inches from her face.

"How did you get this?" Emily asked, walking closer to her.

"Go to hell!" Veronica spat, trying not to look afraid.

Emily's attention turned as the phone began to ring.

"It's for you," Veronica smiled at her.

Emily pushed the phone into her pocket and threw Veronica back into the cell. After making sure the door was locked, she headed out of the security building with Marley. The phone continuously rang in her pocket. The caller was obviously not going to give up any time soon. She reached for her waist and grabbed the walkie.

"Shawn, I need you guys," Emily said into the walkie.

"Where are you?" Shawn's voice came back with concern.

"Security building," Emily answered.

She waited with Marley for only a few minutes before Shawn appeared with the others.

"What happened?" Alec asked, running at her with concern.

"I'm fine," Emily assured him.

The phone in her pocket began to ring once more. Everyone's eyes widened as Emily pulled the phone out of her pocket.

"She wanted to tell me I should answer the phone," Emily said to them. "They had this in their cell."

"How?" Sam asked, stepping forward, anger dripping off him.

"I don't know," Emily said, shaking her head. "I just didn't want to answer it alone."

"We're here," Shawn said, stepping forward.

Emily nodded and answered the phone, putting the call on speaker.

"May I speak to Robert, please?" The General's voice oozed out.

"He's unavailable," Emily replied. "But I'd be glad to take a message."

"It may interest you to know that you are harboring the man responsible for this world," The General replied. "I'd be happy to remove him from your little community in exchange for my daughter."

"I'm talking to the man responsible," Emily replied angrily.

"Is that what he told you?" The General sounded almost happy.

"He doesn't say much these days," Emily replied. "Being dead kind of makes him less chatty."

The line stayed silent, and Emily looked around at everyone.

"I'm not in the mood for games," The General finally spoke. "I want Robert and my daughter before sundown."

"No," Emily replied shortly.

"Then you have no one to blame but yourself," The General replied. "I'll call tomorrow to see if you changed your mind."

The call ended, and Emily returned the phone to her pocket.

"What would make you change your mind?" Cole asked, confused.

"It's mind games," Dillon spoke up.

"It has to be," Shawn nodded. "Let's keep this phone out in case he calls back."

Emily nodded but couldn't help the sick feeling that settled into her stomach. The General had sounded so sure of himself. What could he possibly be thinking would happen?

"The kids are done for the day," Shawn said, pulling her out of her thoughts. "We should probably search the cells and then all head home."

"Let's search the cells," Emily agreed. "But then, let's do something."

Emily looked around at everyone's confused faces.

"We have to live," Emily smiled at Dillon. "And he has slowly been isolating us from each other."

"Party?" Dillon said as a smile spread across his face.

"I'll get the jars," Cole smiled as he turned towards the garage. "You wanna help me, big guy?"

Alec nodded with a smile and turned to follow him. Shawn grabbed his radio and told Sara to announce a get-together tonight. Emily couldn't help but smile as everyone seemed to accept her idea.

"Let's get this over with first," Sam said, walking towards the door.

"This will be fun," Dillon said, rolling his eyes and walking forward.

"Here to let us out?" Veronica grinned as they walked in.

"In a way," Shawn nodded as he unlocked the doors.

Emily grabbed Veronica and forced her hands behind her while Sam put the cuffs on her.

"This isn't necessary," Veronica said as she tried to fight against them.

"Yes, it is, princess," Sam said, pulling her out of the cell and forcing her to sit on the ground.

Emily looked over and saw that Shawn and Dillon had done the same with Chad.

"Where's Steven?" Chad asked, looking around. "We're taking him with us."

"You're not going anywhere," Emily said with a smile as the guys began to search the cells.

"You can't be this stupid," Chad said, glaring at her.

"You're stupid if you think I would let you go and take our son with you," Emily glared back at him.

"There's nothing here," Shawn said, walking out of the cell.

"There wouldn't be," Dillon said, looking down at Chad and Veronica. "They thought they were leaving."

Understanding, Shawn helped Dillon pull Chad and Veronica to their feet.

"Don't touch me!" Veronica yelled as they began to search her.

"This isn't a joy for either of us," Dillon said, rolling his eyes as he continued.

Emily watched Dillon find a piece of paper hidden in Veronica's pocket. Once they were finished, Chad and Veronica were returned to their cells. Emily and Sam followed them back out of the Security building while Veronica yelled a string of obscenities after them.

"What is it?" Emily asked Dillon as soon as they were outside.

Dillon pulled the paper out of his pocket and handed it to her.

"Looks like coordinates," Dillon said as she looked at the numbers. "Probably, where she was supposed to meet daddy."

"We still don't know how she got the phone," Shawn said, looking concerned.

"She's only had it a few weeks," Emily offered. "So, someone had to give it to her."

"Maybe one of the people you let go," Dillon said, looking angry.

"No way," Sam spoke up. "They haven't been allowed near the building.

"But no one watches them at night," Dillon added, looking at him.

"I lock the door myself each night," Sam said, getting frustrated. "And unlock it each morning."

"Maybe one of them is good with locks," Dillon said, standing taller and stepping towards Sam.

"Stop it!" Emily yelled, causing them to back away from each other.

"None of them would have the skills," Shawn said, trying to help calm the situation.

"That means someone else is helping them," Emily said, the words getting caught in her throat.

"I'll make a list of who could get in and out of there," Shawn offered.

"They may be part of the plan for tomorrow," Dillon said, turning his gaze from Sam to Shawn.

"That's tomorrow's problem," Emily interrupted them before they could start working. "Tonight, we have a party."

"I know," Shawn smiled at her. "We should just keep an eye out for anything."

"Let's go," Emily nodded in agreement.

Shawn laughed as he put his arm around her and walked toward where everyone was gathering.

"I actually need to talk to Dillon," Emily said as she stopped. "We'll catch up in a second."

"No working," Shawn warned as he kissed her head.

"No work," Emily promised.

"What's up?" Dillon asked once they were alone.

"Jose had an idea to help you with your nightmares," Emily said softly. "But I wanted to get your permission."

"Okay," Dillon said, eyeing her with suspicion.

"He wants to build a memorial for the people who haunt you," Emily said, looking at him. "That way, they can be remembered."

"You think it will help?" Dillon said, looking at her, the pain evident in his eyes.

"It couldn't hurt," Emily said, not wanting to give him false hope. "He would just need their names and anything you know about them."

Dillon nodded as he stood silent, thinking.

"They deserve it," Dillon said after a moment.

"I'll let Jose know," Emily said softly. "You deserve to find peace, too."

"Maybe just some of that moonshine for tonight," Dillon said with a hopeful smile.

"You talk to Shawn about that," Emily laughed.

Emily walked with Dillon towards where everyone was gathered. The music was already on, and Cole was handing out liquor glasses. Emily stayed towards the edge as Dillon joined them. She watched as everyone relaxed and laughed. This was the Sanctuary she remembered, the Sanctuary she wanted.

"He built it," Shawn said as he wrapped his arms around her. "But you make us a family."

"A dysfunctional family," Emily laughed.

"But still a family," Shawn said, kissing her lightly.

Emily turned her attention back to the people. They never knew each other before the flash and probably never would have. But inside these walls, they were family.

"Let's go," Emily said as she took Shawn by the hand and dragged him into the party.

Shawn followed behind her with a smile as she walked toward Cole. Emily took two glasses from him, handing one to Shawn.

"Half a glass for Dillon," Emily whispered to Cole.

"You sure?" Cole asked, raising an eyebrow at her.

"I'm sure," Emily nodded.

"What was that about?" Shawn asked as they walked away and began to drink.

"Half a glass for Dillon," Emily said as she took a drink.

"He's seventeen," Shawn said with shock.

"And you never drank at seventeen?" Emily eyed him knowingly.

"Well, I…." Shawn replied, trying to figure out what to say.

"He's been through more than we had at that age, and the world is different," Emily continued. "There's nothing wrong with just a taste."

"You continue to surprise me," Shawn laughed, pulling her close.

"And I don't plan on stopping," Emily smiled.

Chapter 5

Emily woke early the following day, her mind content for the first time since her wedding night. Shawn was already gone, probably working on his list of suspects. Emily pulled back the blankets and set to get dressed for the day.

"Mommy!" Steven's voice rang out on the other side of the bedroom door.

"Come in," Emily called back as she sat on the bed to put on her shoes.

"Can we have pancakes before school?" Steven asked before bouncing into the room.

"I think I can do that," Emily laughed as she put on her shoes.

"Where's daddy?" Hope asked as she joined them.

"I think he went to work," Emily smiled.

"But we can't go downstairs," Hope said, plopping down on the bed.

"Why not?" Emily asked, confused.

"Uncle Dillon is still asleep," Hope sighed.

"I got it," Emily assured her as she stood up.

"We're not supposed to," Hope said with a flash of fear in her eyes.

"I'll be careful," Emily assured her as she walked out of the room.

Emily made her way downstairs with Marley and could see that Dillon was still asleep on the couch. However, there were papers scattered across the coffee table. Emily walked closer and picked up one of the papers.

Steven Thompson – Father of 3, wife died on day one. The children's location was unknown. Brown hair, brown eyes. Had a picture of his family in his wallet. Forgive me before I lit the match.

Victoria Taylor – Single woman, midtwenties. An excellent fighter shot for taking down a zombie. Cursed me to hell before I took the shot.

Emily looked through the papers and found similar things written on each. Dillon had written down what he remembered about each of them. Emily set the pieces back on the table and took a few steps back.

"Dillon," Emily called out once she felt she was a safe distance away.

Dillon stirred slightly but soon went still again.

"Dillon," Emily called louder.

"I'm awake," Dillon said as he slowly pulled himself into a sitting position. "Where's Shawn?"

"He left early," Emily explained as she walked closer. "Were you up all night?"

Dillon looked down at the papers and started to gather them up.

"I was up for a while," Dillon said, looking embarrassed. "I didn't hurt you, did I?"

"No," Emily assured him.

"You should have called Shawn to wake me," Dillon said, realizing what had happened.

"It's fine," Emily smiled. "This seems to help."

Dillon nodded as he stood up and stretched.

"You hungry?" Emily asked as she made her way toward the kitchen. "Steven wants pancakes."

"Yeah," Dillon nodded. "I'll be in as soon as I get dressed."

"Tell the kids it's safe," Emily laughed.

"On it," Dillon nodded as he headed upstairs.

Emily opened the back door to let Marley out and set to making breakfast. The kids joined her minutes later and set to doing their chores. She had just finished when Dillon walked in and helped her serve the kids.

"Will you walk us to school today?" Steven asked Dillon with a mouth full of pancakes.

"Sure," Dillon smiled as he tussled Steven's hair.

"We'd better get going," Hope said as she slid out of her chair.

"Right," Dillon said, eating the last of his pancake in one bite and standing up.

"See you guys later," Emily called after them as they headed for the door.

"Love you, mommy!" Hope and Steven yelled just before the door closed.

"Alone again," Emily said, looking down at Marley as he wagged his tail.

Emily patted him on the head as she set to clean up. She had just finished when Shawn came through the front door.

"Emily!" Shawn yelled as he walked through the house.

"Kitchen!" Emily yelled back.

"I don't think it's someone inside the wall," Shawn said, walking in with worry plastered all over his face.

"What?" Emily said, turning towards him.

"The coordinates," Shawn said, holding up the paper. "There to a location on the wall."

"I don't understand," Emily said as fear washed over her.

"I went to the spot, and the plates on the wall look different," Shawn explained.

"Different how?" Emily asked, feeling like she was going to be sick.

"I'll show you," Shawn said quickly. "Do you have the original build plans here?"

"Yeah," Emily nodded, still not moving.

"Emily," Shawn said, taking her by the arms.

"What does this mean?" Emily heard the shake in her voice as she spoke.

"I think someone is coming in," Shawn said.

Emily would have fallen to the ground if Shawn hadn't held her.

"They're getting in," Emily said flatly.

She thought of their army of dead surrounding the wall and couldn't understand how this was possible.

"Maybe," Shawn said. "But if they are, we can stop them. We put some guys at the spot to guard it until we figure this out."

"How could they get passed the zombies?" Emily asked in disbelief.

"We have been noticing more and more wearing uniforms," Shawn explained. "They weren't shot like the others but looked to have been bitten. He could be sacrificing some of his men to allow others to reach the wall."

"They have been coming in like rats while our kids are asleep," Emily said as she got feeling back, only anger, but still feeling.

"They're fine," Shawn assured her as he pulled her close. "We must look at those plans to ensure nothing like this happens again."

"Right," Emily said, straightening herself and walking to the office.

Emily and Shawn pulled out the blueprints and spread them out. They spent hours looking over them, precisely the spot the coordinates indicated.

"There's nothing," Emily said in a huff.

"What's this?" Shawn asked, pulling out a thin piece of rolled-up paper.

"I think it was plans he was working on in case they needed to expand," Emily said after glancing at it.

Shawn unrolled the paper and looked at it for a moment. He then placed it over a blueprint of the wall they had opened. Emily watched him as he lined up the paper. She leaned closer and felt the air get sucked out of her lungs.

"Secret emergency exits," Shawn said as he leaned back. "There are the coordinates." "A door?" Emily said, confused.

"Looks like it was supposed to have a keypad, but he never got to finish it," Shawn said.

"What about the others?" Emily asked, pointing to two other spots on the map.

"We'll check them out," Shawn assured her.

"I'll get Sarah to install the keypad today," Emily said, standing up.

"We will get this taken care of," Shawn said as he stood up to join her.

"Why would he do this?" Emily asked, looking back at the maps.

"It's actually smart," Shawn said, following her gaze. "He wanted a backup plan just in case something happened at the front gate. He just didn't get time to finish."

"His emergency plan ended up putting us all at risk," Emily said, feeling angry with Robert.

"Don't do that," Shawn said, stepping toward her. "Without him, we wouldn't be here."

"We need to get to work," Emily said, pushing the feelings back.

Shawn followed Emily back outside with Marley, and they got to work. There was a tunnel entrance by the farm. It looked to have collapsed at some point, so they didn't worry about it further. There was another secret door on the south side. Sarah quickly set to work and installed security pads on each of them.

"I'll inspect the rest of the wall," Sarah said as she finished. "Just to make sure there are no more."

"Thanks," Emily nodded.

"I'm sorry," Sarah said as she finished gathering her stuff.

"For what?" Emily asked, confused.

"I should have checked the entire wall after I found that one at the front gate she continued. "It was obvious that Robert didn't have time to finish."

"None of us knew," Emily assured her. "I'm just glad you're able to fix it."

Sarah nodded and began working her way around the wall, closely inspecting each section. Emily considered following after her, knowing that she was still blaming herself. Before Emily could decide what to do, her walkie came to life.

"Everyone to the school!" Cole's voice rang out.

Emily didn't hesitate as she took off running as fast as she could with Marley by her side. She made her way back into Sanctuary and kept running hard towards the school. As she neared, she could see that almost everyone was there.

"Mommy!" Steven yelled, running towards her with tears running down his face. Emily scooped him up in a tight hug.

"Where's Hope?" Emily asked, looking around.

"Still inside," Steven cried, hugging her tight.

"What happened?" Emily asked, pulling Steven back and looking at him.

"She stabbed her," Steven cried, falling apart.

"Who stabbed whom?" Emily asked, trying to control herself.

Steven continued to sob and was unable to speak. Emily pulled him close and looked around.

"Cole!" Emily yelled as she ran towards him with Steven in her arms and Marley by her side.

"Emily," Cole came towards her, his eyes heavy with worry.

"What happened?" Emily asked, looking at the school.

"It's June," Cole said with a heavy voice. "She turned in the middle of her class."

"Dear God," Emily breathed as she hugged Steven closer.

"None of the kids were hurt," Cole continued. "But Hope isn't doing well."

"Where is she?" Emily said, looking at the school again.

"With June," Cole said slowly. "She won't let anyone near her.

"Can you watch him?" Emily said as she handed Steven to Cole.

"Shawn's in there," Cole nodded as he took Steven.

Emily took off running with Marley into the school. She quickly made her way to the classroom and saw Shawn leaning against the door.

"Where is she?" Emily asked as she ran towards him.

"She's fine," Shawn assured her as he stopped her before she could reach the door.

"Cole said that June turned," Emily said, confused.

"She did," Shawn nodded. "But she's been taken care of."

"Why is Hope still in there?" Emily asked, trying to push past him towards the door.

"She knows that June was gone," Shawn continued. "But she's never had to put someone down before."

"Hope put her down?!" Emily said in shock.

"She did," Shawn nodded. "With a pencil."

Emily felt like she was going to be sick.

"It was a good thing," Shawn assured. "June could have killed that entire class."

"I need to see her," Emily said, looking back at him.

Shawn nodded and stepped aside. Emily made her way to the classroom and saw June's body still lying on the floor, a pencil stuck in her milky white eye. Just on the other side of her sat Hope, hugging her knees and crying.

"Hope," Emily said as she walked slowly into the room.

Hope didn't move and continued to cry. Emily signaled for Marley to stay as she walked over to Hope. She sat down beside Hope and put her arm around her.

"I'm sorry," Hope cried without looking up.

"You saved the kids," Emily assured her. "June would have wanted you to stop her."

"Howard will hate me," Hope continued to cry.

"No," Emily said softly. "He won't."

"I tried to get her to see Doc," Hope said, lifting her head and looking at June's body.

"What happened?" Emily asked.

"Someone left her a present on her desk," Hope said, motioning to a half-eaten apple. "She joked that she had a secret admirer. But she didn't look so good after she ate a bit of it."

Emily looked at the apple and then back at Hope.

"It happened so fast," Hope cried. "She started coughing and leaned over on the desk. When she stood up, her eyes were just like the monsters. She tried to grab at us, and I…."

Hope broke into another fit of tears and buried her face again.

"We need to get out of here," Emily said to Hope, lifting her face. "The others will take care of her now."

Hope nodded but leaned forward towards June's body. She squeezed June's hand and cried a bit more.

"I'm sorry," Hope whispered before standing up and walking slowly towards the door.

Emily followed Hope outside the room. Hope immediately wrapped her arms around Marley and began to cry once again.

"Where is she?!" Howard's voice rang out in the hallway.

Emily turned to see him running towards them with Sophie in a panic.

"Hold on," Shawn said, stepping forward and stopping him.

"Is she alright?!" Howard demanded, trying to get past him.

"Where's my mom?" Sophie cried, already fearing the worst.

Emily heard Hope begin to sob loudly again. Howard's attention drifted to Hope, and his expression softened slightly.

"Hope?" Howard asked, looking at her with pleading eyes.

"I'm sorry," Hope said, looking up at him with tears streaming down her face.

Howard's strength gave out as he collapsed to the ground and began to sob. Sophie fell beside him and hugged her adoptive father as they cried together. Hope let go of Marley and walked over to Howard.

"I didn't want to," Hope sobbed as she reached him. "But it wasn't her anymore."

"Did she hurt anyone?" Howard asked, not looking up.

"No," Hope said, shaking her head. "I stopped her."

"Thank you," Howard sobbed while holding Sophie.

Emily watched as Howard pulled Hope into his lap, and the two cried together. Shawn walked over to her and put his arm around her as tears began to run down her face.

"If it's okay," Doc said, stepping forward. "I'd like to get her cleaned up before you say goodbye."

Howard nodded, not letting go of Sophie

or Hope. Shawn let go of Emily and followed Doc into the classroom to help. Emily followed behind them slowly.

"The apple," Emily said, looking at the desk. "It happened after she ate the apple."

Doc followed her gaze and looked at the half-eaten apple. Just then, the phone in Emily's pocket began to ring. Emily slowly pulled it out and answered as Shawn walked toward her.

"Has our princess woken from her poison apple yet?" The General's voice oozed out.

"You son of a bitch!" Emily felt herself lose control of her rage.

"Uh, oh," The General gasped. "Did she hurt some little ones?"

"No," Emily snarled, looking at Shawn for support.

"Maybe next time," The General said as if it was no big deal. "Lots of apples."

Shawn grabbed his walkie and said something that she couldn't hear.

"I told you this would be your fault," The General continued. "Deliver Robert and my daughter before more people have to get hurt."

"Robert is dead!" Emily yelled, losing control. "And your daughter is about to join him if you hurt one more person!"

"Then I hope you are ready for your next present," The General said. Emily could almost hear the smile on his face as he spoke.

"The doors are sealed," Emily spat back.

"You figured that out faster than I thought you would," The General replied. "Or was it Shawn who put it all together?" "Doesn't matter," Emily replied, looking at Shawn.

The General was right. It was Shawn who figured it out. However, she couldn't let The General know that. He would take it as a sign of weakness on her part and use it to his advantage.

"How is our boy?" The General asked.

"I'm not your boy!" Shawn said, ripping the phone from Emily's hand. "I'm your worst fucking nightmare!"

Shawn hung up the phone and threw it against the wall. The phone shattered into pieces and then fell to the ground.

"No more talking to him," Shawn ordered as he looked back at Emily.

Emily was taken aback by the anger in his eyes and nodded that she understood.

"They are gathering all the apples in Sanctuary and will destroy them," Shawn continued. "Along with anything else that wasn't locked up."

Again, Emily nodded in agreement. She could tell that he wasn't asking her permission.

Shawn turned and set back to work, helping Doc take care of June. Emily walked out and stood with Howard and Sophie as they carried June's body out of the school. They walked in silence together as they exited the school, where everyone was waiting. Emily knew they wanted an explanation, but her heart was not strong enough to give it. Instead, she walked with Howard and Sophie to the clinic in silence.

"I should get her favorite dress," Howard said once June's body was safely inside.

"I can get it," Emily offered.

"No, we'll get it," Howard said as he turned towards their house.

"Can I come?" Hope asked, reaching for Howard's hand.

Howard smiled slightly with tears running down his face as he took Hope's hand. Emily watched as the three of them walked towards Howard's house. Jose arrived a few minutes later, his eyes red from crying, with a few other men carrying a coffin.

"The grave is almost ready," Jose said as he and the others set the coffin inside.

"Have everyone gather to send her off," Emily said, trying to hold herself together.

Jose left just as Howard and the girls returned carrying a purple dress. Howard and Sophie walked inside and knocked on the door where Doc had taken June. Emily stood with Hope and Marley as Howard handed the dress to Doc. The door closed and reopened a few minutes later. Emily watched as Howard and Sophie entered, and Howard reemerged with June in his arms. He walked over and gently placed June into the casket. Sophie followed him with tears streaming down her face. Cole,

Alec, and Sam walked in. Each took positions on either side of the coffin, with Shawn lifting it into the air.

Emily stepped back with Hope, Steven, and Marley as Howard led them and Sophie out the door with his head held high. Father Nathan followed behind him as they began the walk towards the cemetery. All of Sanctuary walked in silence and gathered between the walls as the coffin was lowered into the freshly dug grave.

"We are here today to say goodbye to our good friend, June," Father Nathan spoke as Shawn and the others stepped back.

Shawn made his way over to Emily and the kids, pulling them all close to him. Emily tried to focus on Father Nathan's words but couldn't. She stood close to her small family and watched as Howard nodded to the words being spoken and held Sophie as she cried.

Father Nathan finished and stepped back. Howard stepped forward and leaned down to the grave where June now rested.

"I love you, sweetheart," Howard cried as he looked down.

"I love you, Mom," Sophie managed to say through thick sobs.

Emily cried as she watched Howard stand up and begin to sing. She didn't know the song but felt it was one of June's favorites. Everyone remained until Howard finished. Howard and Sophie said, " I love you," before walking back towards the gate. Emily waited with her family as everyone said their final goodbye and followed the direction that Howard and Sophie had taken. When everyone was finished, Emily approached the grave with her family. Emily said her final goodbye and waited for her family to do the same.

"This can't happen again," Emily said to Shawn as they walked back.

"I agree," Shawn said without looking at her.

Chapter 6

June's death seemed to make the dark cloud in Sanctuary even thicker. They had decided to cancel classes for a few weeks to give everyone time to mourn. Sanctuary was running with only essential things going. For the most part, everyone stayed inside their houses, the days of playing in the rain long behind them. Hope had nightmares about that day, about having to put June down. Emily and Shawn tried everything to help ease her pain, but nothing worked.

"I'm sorry," Hope's voice sobbed from her bedroom.

"I got her," Shawn said, throwing back the blankets to stand up.

"Can I try?" Dillon said from the doorway, catching them both by surprise. "I've been where she's at. Maybe I can help."

Emily looked at Shawn staring at her. Apparently, it was her decision. Dillon had seemed to overcome his night terrors for the most part. And it was clear that nothing she or Shawn was doing was helping.

"Sure," Emily nodded.

Dillon nodded and walked over to Hope's room. Shawn continued to sit on the edge of the bed, just in case he was still needed.

"Hope," they just barely heard Dillon's voice. "

"I didn't want to!" Hope cried loudly in response.

"I know," Dillon said softly.

"Now I'm a monster!" Hope continued to cry.

"Now that's crazy," Dillon replied. "You could never be a monster."

"I killed her," Hope continued to sob.

"No, you freed her," Dillon corrected her. "The General killed her."

"But I…" Hope began before the sobs became so strong she couldn't speak.

"You want to know how I know you are not a monster?" Dillon asked her softly.

"How?" Hope choked out.

"Because you care," Dillon answered. "You keep reliving the moment, trying to find a way to save her. Monsters don't do that."

Emily sat in shock as she heard Dillon repeating the same thing she told him not too long ago.

"Is that why you used to have nightmares?" Hope asked, her sobs slowing down.

"Yeah," Dillon answered her. "But remembering the people, sharing things about them helped me."

"It did," Hope said.

"Yup," Dillon answered. "Maybe that's what you should do. Share your good memories about June to help keep her memory alive and ensure she's not forgotten."

"With who?" Hope asked, calming down even more.

"Anyone who will listen," Dillon answered. "I'd love to hear some."

"Okay," Hope said, the shake almost completely out of her voice.

Shawn lay back in bed as Hope began to tell Dillon stories about June. Emily had not heard Hope be able to talk in weeks without crying until tonight. Emily listened to Hope talk for hours until she drifted off to sleep. Dillon never returned by the door, and Emily felt confident he was asleep on her floor. She felt herself slowly close her eyes and drift off to sleep for a few hours.

Emily woke early the following day and quickly made everyone breakfast. Everyone was gathered around the table, eating in silence.

"We need to reopen the school," Hope said, causing them all to look up from their plates.

"We will," Emily smiled at her softly.

"When?" Hope asked with irritation in her voice.

"Soon," Emily answered. "Everyone still needs time after what happened."

"We've had time," Hope argued, getting angry. "June would want us in school. She always said it was important and would be angry that she was the reason why we stopped going."

Emily looked at Hope with shock as she spoke. Emily knew that Hope was strongwilled, but this was a lot.

"Maybe we could talk to everyone and see if they're willing," Shawn offered to break the silence.

"I'll talk to Howard," Hope said as she started eating.

"I'm not sure that's a good idea," Emily said cautiously, looking at Shawn.

Howard and Sophie had stayed inside their house since the day of the funeral. Emily had tried to go talk to them a few times, but Howard always refused to open the door for her.

"Can't I at least try?" Hope pleaded with her.

"Okay," Emily said in surrender. "But I don't want you to get your hopes up."

Hope finished her breakfast with a smile of victory on her face. She quickly put her plate in the sink and headed upstairs to get ready.

"You want to hang with me for a while today?" Shawn asked Steven with a smile. "Looks like the girls have some work to do."

"Sure," Steven smiled as he jumped up and ran upstairs to get ready.

"She's a strong girl," Dillon said, seeing the look of worry on Emily's face. "She won't give up until she succeeds."

"I know," Emily sighed.

"That's a good thing," Shawn spoke next.

Emily nodded as she heard footsteps coming back down the stairs. Steven ran into the kitchen and seemed eager to go. Emily quickly kissed Shawn and Steven goodbye and headed outside with Hope and Marley. They made the short walk to Howard's house and arrived in a few minutes. Hope didn't hesitate as she walked straight up to the door and knocked. Emily waited with Marley a short distance behind her. Hope continued to knock for several minutes.

"I don't think he's up to talking today," Emily said to Hope.

"Mr. Howard!" Hope called knocking again. "Mr. Howard!"

Emily couldn't help but be surprised as Howard slowly opened the door. He was a mess and had obviously not been taking care of himself. His face was full of scruff, his clothes were disheveled, and he looked like he had been wearing them for days, and large bags were sagging under his eyes.

"Hope?" Howard said, looking down at the little girl.

"Good morning, Mr. Howard," Hope said in her most comforting voice. "I was wondering if you had some time to talk today?"

"I....Uh," Howard stuttered, looking at Emily.

Emily said nothing as this was Hope's task, not hers.

"What about?" Howard asked, looking back at Hope.

"Mrs. June," Hope said, looking up at him. "It's important."

"I don't know…." Howard said, shifting around awkwardly.

"Please," Hope said, taking his hand as he tried to step back inside.

"Alright," Howard nodded.

"Why don't we talk outside?" Hope said, tugging at his hand. "It is a beautiful day." Howard nodded and stepped out into the day. As far as Emily knew, this was the first time he had stepped outside since the funeral. The light obviously bothered his eyes as he shielded them with his hand while they adjusted.

"Where's Sophie?" Hope led Howard over to the porch swing.

"Upstairs, in her room," Howard replied as he sat down. "She's not feeling well."

"Would it be alright if I checked on her?" Emily asked, stepping forward.

"Of course," Howard nodded, motioning towards the door.

Emily sent Marley over to Hope and stepped inside the house. She had only been here a handful of times, but it was not the home she remembered. Everything seemed dark, and things were scattered everywhere. She quickly made her way upstairs and knocked on Sophie's door.

"Go away!" Sophie's voice came back.

"It's me," Emily answered, trying to hide the concern in her voice. "I just wanted to check on you."

Suddenly, the door to the bedroom swung open, and Sophie looked at her with tears in her eyes. She was just as much of a mess as Howard. She was wearing wrinkled pajamas that looked like she had been in them for days, her hair was a knotted mess, and her eyes were red and swollen from crying.

"How are you doing?" Emily asked. She felt foolish asking, as the answer was evident.

"I can't lose my dad, too," Sophie said, tears spilling from her eyes.

"You won't," Emily said as she pulled the girl into a hug.

"I will," Sophie cried. "He keeps saying he can't live without mom."

"He's just hurting," Emily tried to comfort the girl. "He doesn't mean it."

"Where is he?" Sophie asked, looking around with panic in her voice.

"He's on the porch talking to Hope," Emily said, trying to calm her down. "She had some things she wanted to talk to him about."

"He's outside?" Sophie asked with disbelief.

"Yeah," Emily smiled at her. "Why don't you get cleaned up and come join them?"

Sophie went back into the room, quickly changed into some clean clothes, and even got a brush through her hair. Emily couldn't help but notice the difference as she came back out. They went back downstairs to where Hope and Howard were still talking.

"Dad?" Sophie said as she stepped out into the sunlight, shielding her eyes as Howard had.

"Come here, sweetheart," Howard smiled at her softly as he held a hand to her.

Sophie walked slowly over to Howard and took a seat beside him.

"What's going on?" Sophie asked, looking between him and Hope.

"Hope was just telling me that your mom would have kicked my butt for how I've been behaving," Howard answered as he squeezed Sophie's hand. "I'm so sorry."

"It's okay, Dad," Sophie cried. "I just don't want to lose you, too."

"You're not," Howard said firmly. "I've got too much to do."

"I was just telling Mr. Howard that Mrs. June would be upset that the school was closed," Hope spoke.

"She would be furious," Sophie laughed, tears still in her eyes.

"I'll help get it going again, but the parents would have to be comfortable sending their kids there," Howard said with a look of doubt in his eyes. "Not an easy thing to ask of them."

"We could do something to show them that you support it," Hope offered.

"What do you have in mind?" Howard asked her knowingly.

"The school doesn't have a name," Hope began. "If it's okay with you, I thought we could name it after June. I'm sure Jose would make a sign for us to dedicate on the first day of class."

"She would love that," Sophie said, turning to look at Howard.

"It's perfect," Howard nodded in agreement. "You let me know when the sign is ready, and I will ensure the school is ready."

Hope nodded with a smile of excitement as she hopped off the swing and walked off the porch with Marley. Emily followed them, swelling with pride at her daughter. She may only be three, but she was wise beyond any of them. Emily walked with Hope and Marley to the construction area. She stayed quiet and allowed Hope to talk to Jose about the sign. Jose only glanced at Emily once to confirm that she was okay with the plan, to which Emily nodded. Jose told Hope he could have the sign ready by Monday. Hope said that would be perfect before thanking him and heading back towards the center of town.

"You're doing a good thing, kid," Emily smiled down at her as they walked.

"I'm just trying to do the right thing," Hope replied, staring straight ahead.

"What's wrong?" Emily asked her as she stopped walking and turned Hope towards her.

"I just miss her," Hope said, looking down at the ground.

"Me too," Emily said, pulling her close.

"Is it okay if I tell you some memories of her?" Hope asked, looking up at Emily slowly.

"Of course," Emily assured. "I have some I would like to tell you too."

Hope's eyes lit up as she began to talk. They walked to the bakery and had lunch together. Hope and Emily continued to share stories and laugh.

"You two seem in better spirits today," Julia said as she walked over to them.

"We were just talking about Mrs. June," Hope smiled at her. "Telling memories of her seems to help the pain in my heart."

"Well, let me join this," Julia smiled as she sat down. "I need some help with that pain."

The three talked a while longer while Marley slept on the floor.

"Mrs. Julia," Hope said as their laughter died for a second. "Will you let Bobby come back to school?"

"Are we starting it back up?" Julia asked with a look of pain on her face.

"I talked to Mr. Howard today," Hope explained. "He has agreed it was time, and Mrs. June would be angry if it was still closed." "Yes, she would have," Julia agreed.

"We are going to start again on Monday once the sign is ready," Hope continued.

"Sign?" Julia asked, looking between them, confused.

"Hope has gotten permission from Howard and Sophie to name the school 'June's School," Emily explained. "She met with Jose, arranged for a sign to be made, and arranged a dedication ceremony for Monday before classes."

"That's lovely," Julia smiled with tears in her eyes, looking at Hope. "What can I do to help?"

"I want to put some things out for everyone to remember, June," Hope said after a few minutes. "Maybe some pictures."

"I can talk to Jessica and have some prints made," Julia offered.

"I also want everyone to share memories of June," Hope said, looking down. "Happy memories."

"We could hang a string and put clothespins on it," Julia said after a moment. "Then ask each person to write down their favorite memory of June and clip it to the string. After the dedication, we could gather all the papers and make them into a book."

"Then we could give the book to Mr. Howard and Sophie," Hope smiled.

"I'm sure they would love that," Emily smiled.

"Well, we have a lot of work to do this weekend," Julia said, standing up. "I'll help spread the word about the dedication."

"And Bobby will be at school?" Hope asked, returning to their original question.

"He's driving me crazy anyway," Julia winked at Hope.

"There you two are," Christine said, walking into the bakery. "I just spoke to Howard, who told us the school is reopening on Monday."

"Yup," Hope smiled at him. "It's time we kids started learning again."

Christine looked confused for a moment as she looked between Emily and Hope.

"Hope's taking the lead on this one," Emily smiled as she took a sip of her water.

Emily sat back and listened as Hope explained everything to Christine. Emily felt even prouder as Hope spoke. Christine hung on her every word, nodding and praising Hope as she spoke.

"That is quite a plan," Christine said as Hope finished. "Very well thought out and just what is needed."

"Thank you, Grandma," Hope smiled.

"I will let all of the other teachers know and let us know how we can help," Christine smiled as she stood up.

"I will," Hope grinned as Christine left.

Hope quickly finished her water, and Emily did the same. After a quick goodbye to Julia, they walked back out into Sanctuary. The news of the school opening was already spreading around town. However, Emily was happy that everyone seemed to know Hope was responsible. Many people stopped Hope to tell her she was doing a good thing and ask how they could help. Hope couldn't wipe the smile off her face as they returned home.

"I was wondering when you two were coming back," Shawn grinned at them from the couch. "I heard the princess made her first decree today with great success."

"Everyone really liked my idea," Hope smiled at him.

"So, I've heard," Shawn grinned back. "I'd better get back to work, though."

Emily looked before him and saw that he had been writing something before they came in. There were a few crumpled pieces of paper on the floor, showing that it took him a few times to get it right. Hope walked closer and looked down at the paper.

"I should go get started on mine, too," Hope said as she turned and headed for the stairs.

"Where's Steven?" Emily asked as she sat down on the couch beside Shawn.

"Upstairs writing too," Shawn answered as he continued to write.

"What memory did you pick?" Emily asked, leaning over to look at the paper.

"Our first day here," Shawn answered.

He stopped writing and put his pen down on the table before turning to Emily. She saw tears threatening to fill his eyes as she put her hands on his face.

"It's supposed to be a happy memory," Emily said, looking at him softly.

"It is," Shawn assured her. "I just didn't know it at the time."

Emily looked at him, confused, and waited for him to explain.

"You were still out from the surgery, and even though Doc said you would be fine, I wanted to protect you," Shawn said slowly. "I was sitting in that room for hours, unable to leave you."

"You were still there when I woke up," Emily smiled at him.

"June came in and sat with me for a while," Shawn continued. "She and I hadn't been really close outside the wall, but she was a hard person not to like."

Emily nodded, encouraging him to continue.

"She didn't say anything the whole time until she stood up to leave," Shawn said as he pushed a stray hair behind Emily's ear. "She told me I was lucky to have found you and that she knew we would be perfect together."

"What?" Emily said in shock.

"Yeah," Shawn laughed. "When I told her she was crazy, she smiled and said she'd remind me of that when we married."

"Did she?" Emily asked with a smile.

"Oh, yeah," Shawn laughed. "She walked up to me just before the ceremony and looked me straight in the eye as she told me I told you so."

"That is a good memory," Emily smiled at him.

"I have some others," Shawn said, motioning to the crumpled papers on the floor. "But I think that one has to be my favorite."

Chapter 7

The dedication ceremony went beautifully. Hope worked with everyone, and every detail was perfect. Emily made sure to let Hope take the lead on everything. Hope made an excellent little speech about June just before Jose revealed the new sign. The lines hung around the schoolyard were covered in papers, each telling a memory about June. Jessica had made several pictures that were displayed in front of the school. When it was over, Emily helped take down all the papers, and Jessica took them to make the book.

All the parents had sent their kids back to school. All of them were nervous but still went through with it. Howard had closed off the classroom where June had died. He said it was still too painful for anyone to go in there just yet. Emily agreed with this decision and didn't have plans to reopen it for a long time.

Everything had been quiet inside Sanctuary for a few weeks. Emily was sure that The General had tried to call again. But with the phone destroyed, she had no way of knowing for sure. They still had the one given to Shawn and Veronica originally, but both were powered off and locked up in the armory. Emily could feel the dark cloud that had surrounded them for months begin to lift as life began to breathe into Sanctuary.

"We finished the memorial," Jose said, walking into her office and pulling her out of her thoughts. "Took longer than I hoped, but I wanted it to be perfect."

Emily had nearly forgotten about the memorial for all the people Dillon had been forced to kill for The General.

"I'm sure it is," Emily smiled at him.

"I've got it covered with a tarp until you're ready," Jose continued.

"I'll talk to Dillon and get everything set up," Emily nodded, standing from her chair.

"He seems to be doing better," Jose continued.

"He is," Emily agreed. "I think this is just what he needed."

Jose smiled with pride as he turned and walked out of the office. Emily waited for Marley to stand up from the floor before walking out. Dillon was on wall duty, so she knew where to find him. However, she gathered Julia, Jessica, and Sarah first to help her prepare everything.

"We can do it tonight," Julia said with a confident nod.

"Yeah, we need to get this done not only for Dillon but for all of us," Sarah added.

"We need to be able to fully heal and move past the grieving," Jessica said.

"You're right," Emily nodded. "I'll talk to Dillon, and if he's okay with it, we'll do it."

Emily walked out of the COM building and up the wall. Shawn had been doubling the number of people on duty since June's death. He didn't want to risk The General finding another entrance and getting in. Lucky for her, Dillon was positioned above the gates, so she didn't have to go far.

"Anything?" Emily asked as she and Marley walked up to him.

"Just the dead," Dillon smiled back at her.

"Is it strange that I find that comforting?" Emily laughed, looking out at the sea of zombies.

"We're all a little strange," Dillon smiled at her. "What brings you up here?"

"Jose finished the memorial," Emily said, looking back at him. "If it's okay with you, we wanted to do the unveiling tonight."

"What would I need to do?" Dillon asked, rubbing his neck awkwardly.

"You give a speech if you want," Emily suggested.

She could see immediately that this was not something he was comfortable with.

"I wouldn't really know what to say," Dillon said, looking down. "Sorry, I killed you, but it was to save my own skin."

"You don't have to say anything if you don't want to," Emily comforted him. "But I think that it's important that you are there."

"Yeah," Dillon said, relaxing slightly. "I owe them that much."

"I'll take care of the words," Emily smiled softly.

"Who will be there?" Dillon asked, looking back at her.

"We'll make the announcement and invite everyone," Emily replied. "That way, all those who want to support you have a chance to come."

"It will be a small crowd then," Dillon half-heartedly laughed.

"What matters is that you can do something to help them be remembered," Emily explained. "That way, you can move on."

"Yeah," Dillon nodded, turning his attention back outside the wall.

Emily knew that he was done with the conversation. She made her way back down the wall with Marley. She quickly told Jessica to announce the memorial at seven and encourage all of those who wished to support Dillon to come. As she left the COM building, she could already hear Sarah announcing it over the speakers.

Emily picked up the kids from school and spent a few hours with them playing games before it was time to head to the cemetery. Both of the kids insisted on coming to support their Uncle Dillon. Emily didn't argue as she led them all to the graveyard just before seven.

As they walked around the wall, Emily couldn't help but stop at the sight that awaited them. Everyone in Sanctuary had crowded around, with Dillon standing next to a large object covered with a tarp. Dillon was shifting on his feet, uncomfortable, but seemed to relax when he saw Emily. Emily took the kids by the hand and walked them to where Dillon was standing.

"Why are they all here?" Dillon whispered, looking out at the crowd.

"For you," Emily smiled at him.

"Why?" Dillon whispered back.

"Because we're family," Hope smiled at him as she took his hand. "And family is always there for each other."

Emily nodded in agreement as Steven let go of her hand and went to join Dillon. She walked directly in front of the memorial, and everyone fell quiet. Her eyes fell on Shawn, working his way to the show. She waited until he had joined Dillon and the kids.

"Thank you all for coming," Emily said, turning her attention back to the crowd. "Some of us share, at least in part, the pain that Dillon feels because of The General. The General has found ways to manipulate some of our best by using our hearts against us. Dillon received probably the worst of any of us."

Emily paused as the group began to nod, and some offered looks of understanding to Dillon.

"Dillon was forced through that manipulation to take many lives for The General," Emily continued. "But, each of them lives on through him. Each of their names and faces was etched into his mind. To help ensure that these lives are remembered, Jose and his team worked with Dillon to build this memorial."

Emily turned to look at the memorial just as the tarp fell away. She couldn't help but be taken aback by how beautiful it was. There were several faces carved into it. Based on what she read, it was renditions of some people who died. Written on it were the names and descriptions of each of the people. Across the top was written, "Now a Memory, Forever in Our Hearts." It was positively beautiful to look at.

Emily glanced over at Dillon and could see him staring at the memorial. She couldn't be sure, but there seemed to be tears building in his eyes. She watched as Shawn placed a hand on Dillon's shoulder, and Dillon steadied himself.

"Just because they weren't one of us doesn't mean that their sacrifice should be forgotten," Emily spoke to the crowd once more. "I believe their memory and strength have helped Dillion through the years. And now, we all can share in that with him."

The crowd began to clap, and Dillon looked over them with surprise. The guys from the biker club had been a part of his life before, but everyone else was new. She could see he was taken aback that so many people not only came but supported him.

Everyone waited until they had a chance to shake Dillon's hand. Emily and Shawn stood with him. Each person told Dillon they did not blame him, supported him, and he wasn't alone. Dillon's face remained in shock as each person made their way through. Finally, the three of them were alone in front of the memorial. Marley had gone with the kids back into Sanctuary to play.

"Thanks for saying all that," Dillon said, turning to Emily.

"It was my honor," Emily smiled at him.

Dillon took a few steps closer to the memorial and ran his hands over the carved names.

"How can they all accept me?" Dillon asked suddenly. "I'm a murderer."

"You did what you had to," Shawn said, walking toward him. "No one's hands are clean in this world."

"Not even mine," Emily added as she walked toward them.

"Then how do you know who's evil and who's not?" Dillon asked, looking at them both.

"The good ones care," Emily smiled at him. "They remember."

"I'll never forget them," Dillon said, looking back at the memorial. "I'll fight for each one of them."

"We all will," Shawn assured him.

"We'd better get going," Dillon said with a smile spreading across his face. "Before they eat all the food."

Emily couldn't help but laugh as Dillon walked back towards the gate.

"I hope this is the last time we have to come here for a while," Shawn said as he joined Emily.

"Me too," Emily said, looking around the cemetery.

Shawn kissed her on top of the head as they walked towards the gate. Emily glanced back once more at the three graves and the new memorial. For years, Robert had been the only one out here. Then Charles had been added. But now, they had been out here twice in a month. Deep down, she knew they would be back sooner than she would like. There was still a war brewing outside the wall, and there were always casualties in war.

They walked through the gate to see that Dillon had already found the food. He had a plate filled and was smiling as he ate. He indeed was an excellent young man, despite what The General had tried to turn him into. Emily felt terrible that he was still sleeping on their couch after all this time.

"Maybe we should move him to the apartments," Emily said, looking up at Shawn.

"I talked to him about that today," Shawn replied, meeting her gaze. "He asked to stay a little while longer."

"Really?" Emily said in surprise. "I thought he would be going crazy wanting his own space."

"I think he likes having all of us around for now," Shawn said with a smile. "He likes feeling like part of a family."

"He can stay as long as he wants," Emily grinned at him. "Maybe we could build another room in the basement so he can have some privacy."

"I'll talk to him, and if he's good with it, we'll see what we can do," Shawn nodded, looking back at Dillon, still stuffing his face. "Maybe wait until he's done eating," Emily laughed. She had no idea how Dillon ate so much and stayed so skinny.

"Then I'll never get to talk to him," Shawn laughed as he led Emily over to Dillon.

"You might want to slow down," Emily laughed as Dillon ate half a piece of cake in one bite.

"But the faster I eat, the more I can eat," Dillon said with a mouth full of food.

"We wanted to talk to you about something," Shawn laughed, shaking his head.

"What's up?" Dillon asked before putting the rest of the cake into his mouth.

"We don't think it's a good idea for you to keep sleeping on the couch," Shawn said.

"You want me to move out?" Dillon said with panic on his face after swallowing hard. "Not out, just down," Shawn smiled.

Emily knew that he was purposefully sending Dillon into a panic.

"I don't understand," Dillon said, looking at Emily.

"Stop it," Emily laughed as she slapped Shawn on the arm. "We wanted to know if you would like your own room. We can probably have one built in the basement. That way, you can have some privacy and a bed."

"You serious?" Dillon said as a smile exploded across his face.

"You would have to help build it," Shawn said sternly.

"Yeah, of course," Dillon continued to smile.

"I'll talk with Jose and see what can be done," Shawn said after a moment.

"And I'll get with Jessica to arrange for furniture and stuff," Emily added.

"You don't have to do that," Dillon insisted. "I can take care of it."

"Every place comes with furniture," Emily laughed. "At least the basics."

"I just don't want you guys to have to pay for it," Dillon insisted.

"That's why you are going to help build it," Shawn said. "To help cut down on the cost."

"I will," Dillon nodded. "Thanks for doing this, you guys."

Shawn wasted no time and went straight to talk to Jose. He and his crew showed up the next day. Emily could hear the sounds of construction begin downstairs, but decided to stay out of their way. Jose insisted that they could finish it in a few days.

Emily met with Jessica and was able to make arrangements for the furniture. It would be a hassle to get down the stairs, but that was for Shawn and Dillon to figure out. She went ahead and brought the small stuff home and stored it in her office. She barely used the one at home, so it wouldn't be in the way.

True to his word, Jose and his crew had the bedroom done in just a few days. Emily was surprised at how nice it came out. The walls were painted a clean white, and they had even found the carpet to put down on the cold floor. The full-size bed was already in place, and the dresser was supposed to be here soon.

"Tilt your side to the left," Shawn's voice came from the staircase. "You're other left!"

"That's right," Dillon replied gruffly.

Emily laughed as she walked out of the room and watched the two of them attempting to get the dresser down the stairs.

"Need help?" Emily mused, looking up at them.

"We got it," both Shawn and Dillon replied.

Emily watched as it took them nearly ten minutes to get the dresser into the room. As soon as it was in place, Dillon collapsed on the bed and took a big breath.

"You still got work to do," Shawn said, slapping him on the knee.

"Right," Dillon said, sitting up. "I'll head to the store and get some blankets and…."

"I got most of that in the office for you," Emily interrupted. "You may still want to get some stuff to personalize it, but everything you need is up there."

"I told you I would pay for it," Dillon said, standing up.

"And I didn't listen," Emily said, crossing her arms.

"And you can get your clothes out of the living room," Shawn added, slapping him on the back.

Emily walked with Shawn and Dillon back upstairs. Dillon made his way to the office with his arms full of stuff.

"Can we help?" Steven asked as he and Hope ran over to Dillon.

"I won't stop you," Dillon smiled, nodding back into the office.

The kids took off at a run and began to help Dillon carry everything downstairs. After a few trips, everything had been moved. Emily assumed that Steven and Hope had stayed to help Dillon set up his room.

"That's it," Shawn said as he plopped down on the couch beside her. "The house is full. No more people."

"That's disappointing," Emily smiled at him seductively.

"Okay," Shawn said, pulling her onto his lap. "Maybe one more."

Emily didn't respond as she pressed her lips against his. For the first time in a while, she was happy. Her family was settled, there was no threat knocking on their door, and she could live in this moment. Her thoughts of The General were pushed out of her mind as Shawn pulled her deeper into the kiss.

Chapter 8

The days passed by, with everyone feeling safer and safer. The threat of The General remained a distant memory, and everyone seemed to no longer notice the sounds of the dead outside the walls. Emily felt like herself once again as she walked the streets of Sanctuary. Shawn had kept the extra patrols on the walls, but no one seemed to mind. With their growing numbers, no one had to take a double shift.

Emily had decided to go to the farm this morning. With summer reaching its end, she wanted to ensure Jacob didn't need extra help with the crop. She didn't want to end up in the situation they did last year. Emily walked into the barn to find Jacob tending to Buttercup.

"How's she doing?" Emily asked as she ran her hand over the horse's mane.

"Just as loving as ever," Jacob smiled back at her. "What brings you to my neck of the woods?

"Just wanted to check and make sure you didn't need any extra help," Emily said as she turned to Jacob.

"We are doing okay right now," Jacob nodded. "But I promise to let you know if it changes."

"Good," Emily smiled at him. "We need to be extra careful, considering everything we lost and not being able to go outside."

"I'm on it," Jacob grinned. "No need to worry."

"That's my job," Emily laughed as she turned to leave.

"I do have a question," Jacob called after, causing her to turn back.

"Shoot," Emily said, walking back towards him.

"Are we planning on leaving Chad and Veronica in those cells forever?" Jacob asked.

Emily felt her excellent mood suddenly trying to slip away. She hadn't been to see Chad or Veronica since before June had been killed. She would have rather forgotten about them entirely and let them rot where they were.

"I don't know," Emily sighed. "We can't let them run loose inside, and they are too much of a risk outside."

"What's the risk if we throw them out?" Jacob asked.

"Well…." Emily began.

What was the risk of throwing them out? They had sealed the emergency exits, and Shawn had changed the patrol schedules. No one in Sanctuary would fall for their tricks with the phones anymore. Really, the two of them had no helpful information.

"If they are really a threat, then we should put them out of their misery," Jacob spoke.

Emily looked at him, surprised. He had always been one to argue against putting people down. Hearing him talk about killing Chad and Veronica caught her off guard.

"I'm just saying, keeping them in those cells makes everyone on edge," Jacob continued. "We all deserve a little peace of mind."

"You're right," Emily agreed. "We have a meeting in a few days. I'll get everyone's opinion and make a decision."

Jacob seemed pleased with this answer and went back to brushing Buttercup. Emily turned and walked out of the barn with Marley. She glanced at the fields as she walked. It was always so beautiful here this time of year. It made everything that was going on seem like it belonged in a horror movie.

Emily walked the streets with the empty houses for the first time in years. Most of the places were still open, but that didn't mean they weren't taken care of. Jose and his crew regularly inspected them and made repairs as needed. He told Emily it was because he knew they would be filled one day.

"Emily," Sarah's voice came over the radio.

"Yeah," Emily replied after pulling her walkie from her waist.

"Hey, where are you?" Sarah asked with a twinge of concern in her voice.

"Just walking," Emily casually replied.

"Shawn's looking for you," Sarah spoke again, still concerned. "You're needed on the wall."

"On my way," Emily sighed as she returned the walkie to her waist.

She turned and headed back towards the main street with Marley. Today was just not going to be another good day. Emily reached the wall and quickly made her way up.

"What's going on?" Emily asked as she looked at everyone up there.

"Visitors," Sam said, looking back at her.

"Why didn't Shawn radio?" Emily said, running to look over the edge.

"He kind of lost his temper and broke his walkie," Sam replied.

Emily looked down and saw the same bikers that had been there before, with Clint in the lead. There was also a large SUV with darktinted windows that had not been with them before.

"What happened to the zombies?" Emily asked, noticing the gap in their zombie army.

"They're making a bunch of racket on the south side," Sam replied. "It won't work for long, but it has left this side exposed for now."

"Where's Shawn?" Emily asked, looking back at Sam.

"He took some others to set up a perimeter," Sam answered. "Seemed like a good idea so he could cool off a bit."

"That bad?" Emily asked, looking down at the broken radio pieces.

"He tried to handle it without you," Sam said, glancing back at the people below. "Things got heated pretty quickly."

"That's because he's an asshole," Shawn said, walking up to them. "We're in place just in case they try something."

"Who's in the SUV?" Emily asked, looking back down.

"Don't know, but I have a pretty good guess," Shawn said, gritting his teeth.

"The General," Emily said, looking back at him.

"Did you get them yet?" Clint's voice rang up at them.

"They want Veronica and Robert," Sam explained.

"This again," Emily said, rolling her eyes.

"Robert's dead!" Emily yelled down to Clint. "Killed himself before I found this place."

"You won't like what happens if you don't bring them," Clint smiled up at her.

"What do you want me to do?" Emily gasped. "Dig up his corpse and show it to you!"

Clint turned his head towards the SUV before looking back up at her.

"Veronica," Clint yelled up at her.

Emily felt her anger boil as she was already tired of this game. Jacobs's words echoed in her head. Maybe it was best if she just let them go. She shook the thought from her head. She needed to talk to the council before making that decision.

"Sam," Emily said, turning to face him. "Take Alec with you and bring that bitch up here."

"Are you sure?" Sam asked her, confused.

"I'm sure," Emily nodded before turning back to look at Clint.

"Well?" Clint yelled up at her.

"She'll be here in a minute," Emily yelled.

A sick smile spread across Clint's face. Emily could tell that he felt that this was some kind of victory. In reality, she had a plan to make them all go away. Sam and Alec returned a few minutes later, dragging Veronica, who was kicking and screaming.

"You can't do this!" Veronica yelled as they brought her to Emily.

"Daddy wants to see you," Emily growled as she shoved Veronica closer to the edge.

Emily watched as the SUV door opened, and The General barely stepped out. Emily glanced over at Margaret, who shook her head. Of course, the bastard wouldn't give them a shot.

"Veronica?" The General's voice boomed out.

"Daddy!" Veronica yelled, sounding like a scared child.

"It's alright, sweetheart," The General said more softly. "It will all be over soon."

Emily waited without speaking, hoping that The General would step into a clearer view.

"The kids are in the cellar," Jacob whispered, barely loud enough for Emily to hear.

"Let my family go," The General called up. "Let my family go, and we can find a peaceful way to solve this."

"Like you did with June?" Emily yelled down, trying to contain her anger.

"Is that who ate the fruit?" The General yelled back. "In all honesty, one casualty was not my goal, so you were lucky. There doesn't have to be anymore."

"What are your terms?" Emily yelled back, already knowing they would be ridiculous. "You send out Veronica, Chad, Steven, Robert, and Dillon," The General replied. "Shawn as well. In exchange, we will leave and never return."

"Robert is dead!" Emily screamed, not understanding why no one could understand this.

"He is," Veronica cried. "I saw the grave, and no one is alive here named Robert."

"Fine," The General said, frustrated. "Then send all the others."

"You can have Chad and Veronica,"

Emily replied. "The others stay here."

"I want my family!" The General bellowed.

"They're my family!" Emily replied.

"Daddy?!" Veronica yelled as The General climbed back into the SUV and shut the door.

"You're not really what he wants," Emily whispered into Veronica's ear. "You have no value to him."

As she looked at the SUV, hot tears began to run down Veronica's face.

"You're wrong," Veronica growled at Emily. "He will kill everyone here to get us back."

"We'll take Veronica and Chad," Clint yelled up. "But we aren't done here."

"That's not the deal," Emily spat back.

"Just hurry up and send them down," Clint said, sounding almost bored.

"Fine," Emily shrugged, pushing Veronica closer to the edge.

Veronica let out a scream that caused a few zombies to turn back toward the gate. Emily watched as the bikers were careful to hold back the dead but not kill them.

"What are you doing?!" The General's voice boomed.

"I'll let them go when I'm ready," Emily yelled. "If you want to rush me, this is how it happens."

Emily glanced around and could see everyone staring at her. The stares didn't bother her, but the look of fear in some of their eyes did. She knew that this was a crazy and evil thing to do, but she had no choice. Nothing else was going to get The General's attention. She was done playing around and having her life interrupted every time they showed up.

"Fine," The General yelled.

Emily watched as the bikers climbed on the motorcycles to prepare to leave.

"This was your choice," The General spat before his SUV began to drive away.

"Put her back in her cell," Emily said, shoving Veronica back towards Sam and Alec. "And you keep quiet, or we will finish what we started."

Veronica nodded at her with tears still streaming down her face as Sam and Alec walked her back down.

"Are you alright?" Shawn asked, walking closer to her.

"Fine," Emily replied casually.

"Were you really going to throw her off the wall?" Shawn asked, looking at her, concerned.

"No," Emily said, shaking her head. "I just needed them to believe I would."

"We all believed you," Shawn said, pulling her close.

All of his rage seemed to be gone.

"You know I love you, right?" Shawn said as he pulled her back and looked at her.

"Yes," Emily said to him with suspicion. "Are you worried I'll throw you off the wall?"

"I don't want to risk it," Shawn smiled at her.

"You're safe," Emily smiled back. "I promise."

Emily leaned up to kiss Shawn when a gunshot echoed around them. Emily looked around for the source and then back at Shawn. Usually, he would have knocked her to the ground and told the guards what to do. Shawn was standing still, his face completely free of emotion. Emily watched as blood began to run freely from his chest.

"No!" Emily heard herself scream as she fell to the ground with Shawn.

"Sniper!" Dillon yelled as he fell to the ground beside him.

The sounds of everyone ducking were missed by Emily as she placed her hands over the gunshot wound.

"A few inches lower, and they would have gotten you, too," Dillon said as he looked at Shawn. "We need to get him down."

"Shawn," Emily cried, not hearing his words. Shawn's eyes were glued to hers, but he could not speak.

"We got him," Alec said as he pulled her back and took her spot.

Emily watched as they dragged Shawn to the stairs and carried him down. She looked down at her blood-covered hands, her eyes blurry with tears. This was her choice. The General's words echoed in her head. The shot wasn't meant for Shawn. It was meant for her, only off by a few inches.

"Emily," Sarah said softly, crawling over to her. "Emily, we need to get down."

Emily looked up with tears in her eyes, unable to speak.

"Come on," Sarah said as she pulled her towards the stairs.

Emily followed her down with little thought, almost like she was on autopilot. She leaned against the wall as soon as they reached the bottom and sank to the ground. She looked at her hands, still covered in Shawn's blood.

"Get some water," Sarah said to someone.

Emily couldn't even look up to see who brought the water. Sarah immediately started washing Emily's hands, the water turning red and pooling on the ground.

"What happened?" Joe said as he ran up to them.

"A sniper," Sarah said as she wiped Emily's hands. "Shawn's in bad shape."

"Is she hit?" Joe asked as he began to look her over.

"She's in shock," Sarah replied.

"Emily," Joe said, trying to get her to look at him.

Emily's eyes remained fixed on the red water pooled before her. It was beginning to run away, leaving a red stain as it traveled. Her husband's blood, Shawn's blood.

"We need to get her up," Sarah said to Joe.

"Right," Joe said as he grabbed Emily in his arms. "Someone needs to get the kids."

"Julia's got them," Sarah said as she led them through a doorway. "Set her down there."

Emily felt Joe set her down in a chair and use his hands to steady her.

"It's going to be okay," Joe assured her, but Emily did not register his words.

"Where is she?" Dillon's voice rang out as he came into the room.

"Right here," Joe called over to him.

"Emily," Dillon said as he walked over and kneeled beside her.

Emily didn't acknowledge him. She knew why he was there. He had come to tell her that her husband was dead, that she had killed him.

"Shawn's with Doc now," Dillon slowly explained. "He's strong. He's going to be okay."

"Is that what Doc said?" Emily heard herself finally speak. "Or what do you hope?"

"It's what I know," Dillon said, trying to catch her gaze.

"It's what we all know," Joe added, still holding onto her shoulders. "You two have been through too much for you to lose him now."

Emily remained silent and ignored their words. She was never meant to be happy. She wasn't supposed to be alive right now. If she had died the day she was bitten, none of this would be happening.

"She needs time," Sarah said, stepping closer. "We should get her home."

Joe nodded in agreement as he picked up Emily once more. She could feel everyone looking at her as he carried her up the street and into her house. Emily didn't care, though. None of them could blame her more than she blamed herself. She felt Joe lay her on the bed. She immediately reached over and grabbed Shawn's pillow, holding it close to her chest.

"You're safe."

Emily heard herself saying the words to Shawn just before the gunshot. Those would be her last words to him. Emily felt the urge to cry, but no tears came. Instead, she lay still, holding his pillow.

"She shouldn't be alone," Sarah said, sitting beside her. "At least not right now."

"Dillon, why don't you get to the clinic to wait for any update?" Joe said. "We'll stay with her."

Dillon didn't say anything, but the sound of his steps told Emily he had left. She knew she should be the one at the clinic waiting for news. It is what any good wife would have done. But she wasn't a good wife. She was the reason her husband was dying.

Emily had no idea how long Sarah and Joe sat with her, but it must have been hours. At one point, Sarah drifted off, but Joe stayed awake and alert. He never let go of Emily and kept assuring her that everything would be fine.

"Emily," Doc's voice came into the room. "How's she doing?"

"Same," Joe answered, standing up. "How's Shawn?"

"He's not out of the woods yet," Doc admitted. "I was able to close the wound, but there is a chance I missed something and could have to go back in."

"Is he awake?" Joe asked.

Emily felt her heart jump into her throat at the question.

"No," Doc said, shaking his head. "But that's not the biggest problem.

"What is it?" Joe asked with concern and urgency in his voice.

"We know why the sniper aimed for his chest," Doc said slowly. "The bullet was coated in the virus."

"THE virus?!" Joe said with shock in his voice.

"Shawn's immune to the airborne, but this was put directly into his bloodstream," Doc explained.

"Can't you give him your antidote?" Sarah asked, moving closer to Doc.

"We tried," Doc said with regret in his voice. "But with this being direct contact with the virus, it has no effect."

"There has to be something else we can try," Joe said as he began to pace around the room.

"I have an idea, but it's a long shot," Doc said hesitantly.

"What?" Joe said as he stopped and turned to Doc.

"He lost a lot of blood," Doc began. "He is going to need several more transfusions."

"Okay," Joe said, irritated, trying to get Doc to explain faster.

"I know everyone's blood type from running the tests," Doc continued. "He and Emily are a match."

"I don't understand," Joe said, looking over at Emily.

"There is a chance that if she were to provide the blood, his body might be able to fight the virus," Doc finished.

"How much blood?" Joe asked with concern.

"Doesn't matter," Emily said, sitting up from her pillow and holding out her arm. "Take it all if you have to."

Chapter 9

Emily walked with Doc into the small lobby of the clinic. She barely glanced up from her feet but could see that people had crowded in. She followed Doc towards the surgery room door and waited as he closed it behind her.

"Have a seat," Doc said softly as he guided Emily to a chair.

Emily sat in the chair and could tell she was next to the operating table, the same table that Shawn must be resting on. Doc had told her he was keeping him here until he was out of danger to avoid moving him more than they had to.

"Are you sure about this?" Doc asked, standing in front of her.

Emily forced her eyes up from the floor and looked over at the operating table. Shawn had a large bandage on his chest, but a stain of pink could be seen peaking through. His skin was a pale white, and his forehead was covered in sweat. Emily found herself reaching for his hand. As she grasped it, she couldn't help but tear up.

"Take it all if you have to," Emily said, holding her arm out to Doc.

"That shouldn't be necessary," Doc assured her as he pressed a needle into her arm.

Emily didn't flinch and remained still while Doc worked. He used a tube to attach the needle in Emily's arm to the needle that was already in Shawn's. Emily watched as the warm, red blood flowed from her into Shawn.

"We only do this for a bit and then take a break," Doc explained. "You must keep hydrated and eat, as he will probably need more."

Emily nodded but kept her gaze on Shawn. She had seen him injured before, but not like this. He looked like there was no life left in him. He looked weak. With her free hand, Emily reached up and brushed the hair off his forehead. Despite the coldness of his hand, she could feel the heat radiating from his head.

"The fever is starting to set in," Doc explained, seeing the worry on her face.

"Am I too late?" Emily asked, looking at him with concern.

"No," Doc assured her. "It hasn't spread at all. This still has a strong possibility of working."

Emily nodded and turned her gaze back to Shawn.

"You're safe," Emily whispered to him.

She sat with Shawn until Doc stopped the blood flow and disconnected the tube.

"That's plenty for now," Doc said as he put a bandage on her arm. "You remember what I said about eating and drinking."

Emily nodded that she did.

"Try to get some rest as well," Doc said softly. "You need to be strong right now."

"He's my strength," Emily said, looking back at Shawn.

"You need to be strong for him," Doc clarified.

Emily looked back at him and nodded.

"You go home now, and I'll let you know if there is any change," Doc said as he checked Shawn's vitals.

Emily squeezed Shawn's hand one more time before heading for the door. The waiting room was still crowded, and Emily forced herself to look straight at the door. She could still feel all their eyes on her as she walked.

"How is he?" Will asked, walking up to her.

"Doc says he's stable for now, but the virus…."Emily's voice failed her before she could finish.

Will looked down at the bandage on her arm and put his arm around her.

"He'll pull through," he assured her.

"I'm supposed to eat," Emily heard her voice say. "Just in case he needs more. I have to be strong for him."

"And we'll be strong for you," Margaret said.

Emily looked around and could see Margaret sitting in one of the chairs.

"Us sitting here isn't going to make him heal any faster," Margaret continued. "We all have jobs, and we need to do them. Otherwise, he will have nothing to wake up to."

Everyone in the room nodded in agreement, and Emily could see the look of determination on their faces. She wished she could share their fighting spirit, but couldn't will herself to do it.

"Let's get you home," Will said as he led her towards the door. "I'm not as good a cook as Shawn, but I make a mean sandwich."

Emily could feel the smile on his face as he spoke, but felt nothing. She walked with him slowly towards her house and sat down in the kitchen. After a few moments, Will slid a sandwich in front of her with a glass of water. Emily quickly ate and drank and waited while Will cleared the dishes. When he finished, Will walked Emily to the couch and sat her down.

Suddenly, there was a scratching at the door. It sounded almost like someone was trying to claw their way through it. Will looked at Emily and walked to the door. He listened for a moment and slowly opened it, looking ready for a fight. As soon as the door cracked, it was shoved the rest of the way open, and Marley came running inside. He ran straight to Emily and jumped on the couch, resting his head on her lap.

"Damn dog!" Will cursed as he closed the door.

Emily said nothing as she slowly ran her hand over Marley's head. Marley remained still, not caring about Will cursing him. Neither

Marley nor Emily moved when the door opened again a few minutes later.

"How's she doing?" Dillon asked, walking into the room.

"Quiet," Will replied, looking over at her. "How are the kids?"

"They are staying with their grandparents," Dillon explained. "But he took off as soon as I opened the door to come back."

"She was right about him," Will said, looking at Marley. "He is special."

"They are trying to organize the security out there," Dillon said, motioning towards the door. "But there is a fight as to whether people should be on the wall or not."

"Of course, they shouldn't be," Will said with frustration. "Especially not tonight."

"I'll take care of her if you want to take care of that," Dillon offered.

"Let me know if she needs anything," Will said after looking at her for a moment.

"I will," Dillon nodded as Will left.

Emily continued petting Marley silently, and Dillon sat beside her.

"The kids are worried about you," Dillon said beside her. "I told them you just needed a night."

Emily didn't respond and kept petting Marley. They sat silently for a few hours before Doc came through the door. Emily lifted her head and looked at him with tears, fearing the worst.

"I had to go back in," Doc explained, looking at her. "It's alright now, but he could use another transfusion if you're up to it."

Emily nodded and slowly stood up from the couch. Marley jumped down, and Dillon stood to follow her.

"Did you eat?" Doc asked her as they walked to the clinic.

"Yes," Emily replied, looking at the ground. "I had a sandwich and some water."

"Good," Doc sighed in relief. "We won't be able to do this one as long."

"Do as long as you need," Emily said with no emotion.

Dillon grabbed onto Marley's collar and forced him to wait while Emily walked with Doc back into the surgery room. Shawn was lying on the table just as he had before, but his bandage was crisp white. Doc must have put it on just before he came to get her. Emily sat back down in the chair and held out her arm. She waited for Doc to remove the bandage and hook up the tube while she held Shawn's hand. It only took a few minutes for the blood to begin flowing again.

Shawn's hand felt slightly warmer than last time, and his head was cooler. Emily still refused to get her hopes up.

"His fever started going down as soon as you left," Doc explained while checking Shawn's vitals. "That's a good sign."

"Will he need another surgery?" Emily asked, still looking at Shawn.

"I don't think so," Doc assured her. "However, we will wait until tomorrow to move him, just in case."

"Will he need more blood?" Emily asked.

"Probably," Doc said. "But we can do those in the recovery room as well."

Emily nodded and remained silent as Doc continued to monitor Shawn. After a few minutes, he came over, stopped the blood flow, and bandaged her arm. Emily went to stand and felt everything begin to spin around her. Doc caught and held her up until she was steadily on her feet.

"You need to rest," Doc said to her as he loosened his grip.

"I can't," Emily sighed, looking at Shawn.

"If you don't rest, you won't be able to give more blood," Doc said sternly.

"Take what he needs," Emily said with anger in her voice. "I don't care if it kills me!"

"I'm not going to kill you to save him," Doc said with authority. "He wouldn't want that, and he would kill me for doing it."

Emily looked at him with hatred in her eyes. She didn't care what Shawn would have wanted. This was her fault, and she would save him no matter what.

"If you want to continue giving him the blood," Doc said, staring back at her unphased.

"You will do as I say." "Fine,"

Emily growled back.

Doc had never ordered her around like this, and she didn't like it. Now was not the time to try to tell her to do anything. Doc remained unfazed, though, as he walked to the door.

"Make sure she goes to bed when she gets home," Doc instructed Dillon. "She can't give him any more unless she has six hours of sleep."

"Yes, sir," Dillon said in almost a military tone.

This angered her even more to hear him talk this way. Marley walked over to her and tried his best to get her attention.

"I'll radio in the morning," Doc continued talking to Dillon. "And if she hasn't slept, we will have to give him different blood."

"That won't stop the virus!" Emily screamed at him.

"We'll just have to hope he's received enough of your blood," Doc said coldly. "Or you could just rest and save us the hassle."

Emily felt her fists clench by her side. Marley stiffened beside her and looked between her and Doc, confused. Dillon shared in Marley's confusion as he stood silent.

"I don't want to fight," Doc sighed, his expression softening. "Just ask yourself, what does he want you to do? Would he want you to kill yourself on a chance it would save him, or try to save him but still make sure at least one of you is here for those kids?"

Emily felt her fists relax as she looked at Doc. She had refused to think about the kids during this whole thing. She was ready to die for Shawn if needed. If she died in a fight, that was one thing, but if she killed herself, it was another.

"I'm sorry," Emily said, feeling ashamed. "I'm just scared."

"We all are," Doc assured her. "It's been a long day, and we still have a few more long ones left."

"Please call if anything changes," Emily said, walking forward with Marley.

"Where are you going?" Dillon asked.

"Home," Emily replied softly. "Doc said I have to sleep."

Emily could see the look of relief wash over Doc's face. Dillon followed her and Marley outside. When they returned home, Emily quickly got a glass of water from the kitchen and headed to her room. Dillon had disappeared to the basement, and Emily assumed he was also going to bed. Emily crawled into bed and pulled Shawn's pillow close to her once more. Marley joined her on the bed and lay where Shawn normally would.

"I'll be okay," Emily said to him as she felt tears run down her face.

Marley huffed where he lay, showing her he did not believe her. Emily reached over and gently patted his head. Someone started making noise outside her door, which caused her and Marley to look. Dillon was in the hall, laying a blanket and pillow on the floor.

"What are you doing?" Emily asked, looking at him, confused.

"I have to make sure you sleep at least six hours," Dillon explained as he sat down.

"So, you will sit and stare at me all night?" Emily couldn't help the slight smile that spread across her face.

"Of course not," Dillon said, rolling his eyes. "I'm not a creeper."

Dillon leaned his head back against the wall and closed his eyes. Emily knew he wasn't going to sleep, but did not have the strength to fight him. She turned her gaze back to Marley, who had also closed his eyes.

"I should do the same," Emily said to herself as she closed her heavy eyelids.

Emily was awakened the following day by Dillon softly shaking her arm.

"What happened?" Emily said as the events of the day before flooded her mind.

"You've been asleep for a while," Dillon smiled at her. "But Doc said I should get you up and let you eat."

"How long have I been out?" Emily said, looking around the room.

"More than six hours," Dillon grinned. "Once you eat, Doc said we should come by the clinic."

"Is he awake?" Emily asked, jumping off the bed with Marley.

"No," Dillon said, shaking his head. "But I helped move him to the recovery room this morning. He looks a lot better compared to yesterday.

Emily quickly grabbed a fresh change of clothes and ran into the bathroom. When she came back out, Dillon and Marley were both gone. She ran downstairs to find Dillon in the kitchen and the back door open. Dillon must have let Marley out and was now filling his food.

"Breakfast is ready," Dillon said to her, nodding at the plate on the counter.

Emily grabbed it and quickly ate the eggs and toast he had made for her. Marley returned while she was eating and quickly ate his breakfast.

"Thanks," Emily said to Dillon as she put her plate in the sink.

"Don't forget the orange juice," Dillon said, handing her a glass. "Doc said it would help."

Emily took the glass and quickly drank it. Orange juice wasn't her favorite, but she would do what she had to right now.

"I'm ready when you are," Emily said as she added the glass to the sink.

Dillon followed her and Marley as they made their way to the clinic. Doc was waiting for them in the waiting room when they entered.

"How are you feeling?" Doc asked her as soon as they walked in.

"Much better," Emily nodded.

"No more dizzy spells?" Doc asked her.

"No," Emily said, shaking her head.

"She ate breakfast and drank the orange juice, too," Dillon added as he sat down.

"Well, if you're feeling okay, we can do another transfusion," Doc nodded. "But you must tell me if you start feeling weak or dizzy."

"I can do that," Emily nodded.

Doc smiled as he turned and led Emily to the recovery room. Emily stopped and stared at Shawn as soon as she walked in. Dillon was right. He looked better than the day before but wasn't back to normal. Some of the colors had returned to his face, and his head was no longer covered in sweat droplets. Emily walked over to the chair beside the bed and took his hand. Doc quickly started attaching the tube, and the blood began to flow again.

"Any change?" Emily asked, looking at Shawn.

"His fever is gone," Doc said. "And this will probably be the last transfusion he needs."

"What about the virus?" Emily asked, looking at him.

"It's still showing in his blood, but the amount is less than it initially was," Doc nodded.

"Does that mean it's working?" Emily asked, allowing herself to feel hopeful.

"Maybe," Doc said with defeat. "Or it could be because more blood is in his system now, so it thinned out. We will know more when I rerun the test this afternoon."

Emily nodded and turned her attention back to Shawn. Doc remained silent and allowed her to sit with him for a long time.

"I'm starting to feel a little sick," Emily said, turning to Doc.

Doc nodded and came over and stopped the blood.

"Did he get enough?" Emily asked while Doc bandaged her arm.

"Yes," Doc smiled at her. "And thank you for admitting you didn't feel well."

"I have two kids to take care of," Emily said as she stood up.

"That you do," Doc nodded.

"Thank you, by the way," Emily said, standing up from the chair.

"I can't say for sure if this is going to work or not," Doc said, looking at Shawn.

"No," Emily said, shaking her head. "Thank you for kicking me in the ass last night." Doc looked both confused and ashamed.

"I was out of my mind," Emily continued. "I need someone to remind me of what I have to do. So, thank you."

"Let's agree next time. It won't be me," Doc smiled. "Don't forget, I'm the one who had to reset Derrick's nose when he made you angry."

Emily couldn't help the smile that crossed her face at the memory. It seemed so long ago now.

"Why don't you go see those kids of yours and get something to eat?" Doc smiled back at her. "I'll let you know when the test results are ready."

Emily nodded and walked back out into the waiting room. Dillon and Marley were still waiting for her, but had been joined by Will.

"Any news?" Will asked. "He looked better this morning, but…."

"We won't know until Doc runs another test this afternoon," Emily explained.

Will nodded and shifted uncomfortably.

"How did things go last night?" Emily asked, referring to the guard duty.

"Alec and I are sharing Shawn's job until he's back on his feet," Will explained. "We kept everyone off the wall last night and plan to do the same today."

"We should wait at least a few days before starting watches again," Emily stated.

"I will let Alec know, and we will do our best to keep everyone busy for the next few days," Will nodded as he walked out of the clinic.

"What now?" Dillon asked.

Emily couldn't help but notice that the look on his face had soured as she talked to

Will. However, she knew not to push Dillon into talking about anything.

"Let's go get the kids," Emily nodded. "There's nothing more we can do right now."

"I can get them if you want to stay here," Dillon offered.

"I'll go crazy," Emily said, looking around the waiting room. "And I can't stop again."

Dillon nodded and opened the door for her and Marley to head out. She was proud of herself for what she had done today. Doc was right. She needed rest. It allowed her to put on the face that everyone needed to see. But that did not change her turmoil, ripping her apart inside.

Chapter 10

Emily spent the rest of the morning with Dillon and the kids. Her family didn't ask her a bunch of questions, and she was grateful. She did not know how often she could explain that they did not know anything yet. Steven and Hope waited until they sat down to lunch to start with their questions.

"How's daddy?" Steven asked, looking up from his uneaten sandwich.

"He's resting," Emily replied with a fake smile.

"Can we see him?" Hope asked with hesitation.

An image of Shawn lying in a hospital bed flashed into Emily's mind. While he did look better than yesterday, he still did not look well. She looked at each of their faces as a struggle raged inside her. She understood them wanting to see him. But she didn't know if he was going to make it. Did she want that to be how they last saw him? It would be their final memory of him.

"Not yet," Emily replied after a few moments of thought.

"Why?" Hope asked firmly.

Emily could tell she was not happy with the decision. However, this was something Emily would not change her mind on.

"I said no," Emily said firmly.

Emily could see the anger in Hope's eyes and the hurt in Steven's.

"As soon as he wakes up, you guys can see him," Emily continued.

"What if he doesn't?" Hope asked, glaring at Emily. "We want to see him!"
"I said no," Emily said firmly.

It took all her strength not to yell back at Hope. She knew that Hope and Steven wanted to see their dad. But she wouldn't let their last memory be of him in a hospital bed.

"Now, finish your food," Emily said, looking back at her lunch.

"I'm not hungry," Hope spat as she pushed back her chair.

Emily said nothing as Hope ran upstairs to her room.

"I'm not hungry either," Steven said with tears.

"Can you try to eat just a little for me?" Emily pleaded with him in a soft voice.

Steven nodded and slowly took a few bites.

"Thank you," Emily smiled as he finished and got up from the table.

"May I go check on Hope?" Steven asked.

"Of course," Emily nodded at him.

Steven ran out of the kitchen and upstairs to find Hope. Emily forced herself to finish her lunch.

"That was intense," Dillon said as she cleaned up.

"I just can't let that be their last memory of him," Emily sighed as she walked towards the sink.

"He's going to be fine," Dillon assured her as he began to help.

"We don't know that yet," Emily said, fighting back the tears.

"Emily," Doc's voice came over the radio. "The results are in."

"Sounds like we will in a minute," Dillon said hesitantly.

"Can you watch the kids for a minute?" Emily asked as she turned to leave with Marley.

"I got them," Dillon nodded.

Emily walked outside with Marley and quickly made her way to the clinic. She was both nervous and excited about hearing the results. She paused as her hand reached out for the clinic door. She didn't know if she could handle it if the virus was spreading, if her blood didn't work. Marley nudged her side, and Emily walked through the door. Emily made her way to Shawn's room after telling Marley to stay in the waiting room.

"How is he?" Emily asked as she walked in.

"Still unconscious," Doc said to her while writing on a clipboard.

Emily went to sit in her chair and took Shawn's hand. It was warmer than it had been this morning.

"You said the test was done," Emily said, looking at Doc.

"Yes," Doc nodded. "There are still traces of the virus, but they appear dead."

"What does that mean?" Emily asked, trying to keep herself from getting excited.

"It's similar to how your blood looks after you've been bitten," Doc explained.

"So, it worked," Emily said, looking at Shawn in surprise.

"It appears so," Doc nodded. "But there is a problem."

"What?" Emily said, snapping her eyes back to him.

"The levels of the dead virus in his blood are triple what yours were when you went into your coma," Doc explained.

"I don't understand," Emily said, looking back at Shawn.

"You were in your coma until your body could get rid of all of it," Doc continued. "With Shawn's being even higher and his body not built to fight it…."

"You can't know if he'll wake up," Emily said in defeat.

"I will keep running the tests every day, and we will just have to wait," Doc said, walking closer to her. "He's already done better than we could have hoped. If anyone can get through this, it's him."

"Is he in a coma now?" Emily asked with tears in her eyes.

"I don't know," Doc said slowly. "I have him on medication to keep him asleep due to his injury. I'll take him off it in a few days, and then we'll know for sure."

Doc placed his hand on her shoulder before turning and leaving Emily alone with Shawn. Emily remembered her coma vividly. There were times when she was trapped in darkness, but she could also hear everything around her. She could listen to everything but couldn't respond to anything. If Shawn were in the same type of coma, he would live in that hell now.

"I'm here," Emily cried as she squeezed his hand. "But you can't give up. You have to fight."

Shawn didn't respond, and Emily hadn't expected him to.

"I need you," Emily cried, laying her head on his shoulder. "I love you."

Emily stayed with Shawn a while longer. She knew it was getting late, and she should get home.

"I'll be back tomorrow," Emily said as she stood and kissed Shawn's forehead.

Emily put her strong face back on as she walked out of the room. Marley was still waiting for her in the lobby. They walked into the street together to find several people waiting for them. Emily looked at Will, Sam, Cole, and Alec.

"How is he?" Will asked Emily.

"He still hasn't woken up," Emily said as firmly as she could.

"And the virus?" Cole asked next.

"The blood killed it," Emily said, trying to fight the burning feeling in her eyes.

"So, he'll be fine?" Sam asked, sensing that something wasn't right.

"We don't know," Emily sighed. "It's like when I went into that coma. His body has to push out the toxins."

"But he's got your blood, so it should work," Alec said with a smile.

"His toxin levels are three times higher than mine ever were," Emily said. "We don't know if his body can push it all out."

"What can we do?" Will asked, stepping forward and hugging her.

"Wait," Emily replied, hugging him back. "All we can do is wait."

"He'll be fine," Cole said as he stepped forward and hugged Emily. "You two get out of more shit than a dung beetle."

Emily couldn't help but smile at the imagery as she hugged him. Emily hugged both Alec and Sam next.

"I'd better get home," Emily said, looking at them. "Unless you need something from me?"

"We're good," Sam assured her. "You just take care of yourself and those kids."

"I will," Emily nodded as she began to walk home with Marley.

Emily opened the door and entered the house. The living room was empty, and everything was quiet. The kids were probably still upstairs, mad at her for her decision. Emily walked over to the couch and sat down.

"How'd it go?" Dillon asked, walking in from the kitchen.

"The blood killed the virus," Emily sighed. "Now, we must wait and see if he'll wake up."

"Then we're halfway there," Dillon smiled at her.

"I hope so," Emily replied. "How are the kids?"

"Hope is still furious," Dillon said, shaking his head. "Steven is sad."

Emily ran her hands through her hair in frustration. She didn't know how to help them through this. She felt confident she was making the right decision, but hated to see them both in pain.

"Maybe you should let them see him in a few days?" Dillon suggested. "I know you don't want it to be their final memory of him, but I think they need it."

Emily looked at him, confused.

"I didn't get to see my father for years," Dillon continued. "When I finally did get to see him, it was at his funeral. The only solid memory I have of him is in his casket."

Emily looked at him in shock. She had not thought about that.

"As soon as his body heals up a bit more, I'll take them," Emily said, looking upstairs.

"If you've got a moment, I did want to talk to you about something else," Dillon said, looking at her thoughtfully.

"Of course," Emily replied.

"You were talking about putting patrols back on the wall in a few days," Dillon said slowly.

"Yeah," Emily nodded.

"I don't think that's a good idea," Dillon blurted out. "His snipers are some of the best. Sometimes they would camp out for months to pick off people."

"You don't think the shooting was a onetime thing," Emily said slowly.

"I think he's waiting for you to relax and then will shoot more people," Dillon continued. "It's his pattern."

"I trust you," Emily said as she began to think.

"What if we put people in between the plates?" Emily asked. "Just in case there are any more exits that we don't know about, or they try to force their way through one."

"They would be safe there," Dillon said after a moment. "And not something he would expect."

Emily waited while he thought. Dillon had more knowledge of The General than any of them. She would trust what he said concerning this matter.

"I think it's a good idea," Dillon said after a minute.

"I'll let Will and Alec know in the morning," Emily nodded.

Dillon seemed happy with how the conversation went. Emily could see the sour look that had been on his face disappear. This must have been what was bothering him at the clinic that morning.

"I'd better talk to them," Emily said, turning her gaze back towards the stairs.

"Good luck," Dillon grinned as he stood up and returned to the kitchen.

Emily forced herself off the couch and made her way upstairs with Marley behind her. Emily stopped just outside Hope's door, which was barely cracked open.

"You can't be mad at her forever," Steven was pleading with Hope.

"Yes, I can," Hope said firmly.

Dillon was right. She was furious. Emily took a deep breath and slowly pushed the door open.

"Can we talk?" Emily asked as she walked in.

"Have you changed your mind?" Hope spat back at her.

"Yes," Emily said slowly. "But it will still be a few days before you can see him."

"Why?!" Hope yelled. "You got to see him yesterday and today!"

Emily felt a pain in her heart as Hope yelled at her. The kids knew that Shawn was injured, but neither knew what had happened or how bad it was. Hope believed that Emily was just visiting Shawn when she went to the clinic.

"I wasn't visiting," Emily said, sitting down on Hope's bed beside them.

"Then what were you doing?" Hope said in frustration. "Why will no one tell us what's happening?"

"I'll tell you if you really want," Emily said, looking at them. "But I warn you, it's not easy to hear."

Hope's expression softened as she looked at Steven. They nodded to each other and then looked back at Emily.

"The General came and asked me to give him some people," Emily explained. "I refused, and he left. After he left, I heard a gunshot." Emily paused as the words got caught in her throat.

"I looked around to check on everyone, and when I looked back at your dad…."

Emily couldn't help the sobs that broke off her words.

"Daddy was shot?" Steven said with a look of horror on his face.

"Right here," Emily nodded, pointing to a spot on her chest.

The kids waited patiently as Emily worked to slow her sobs.

"They got him to the clinic, and Doc worked hard to fix him up," Emily continued. "But Daddy lost a lot of blood." "Were they able to give him more?" Hope asked with a flash of panic in her eyes.

"They needed special blood, though," Emily nodded. "You know the sickness that makes people's bodies walk around when they die?"

"You can catch it if they bite you," Steven nodded.

"The bullet that shot Daddy was covered in it," Emily replied. "So your dad was starting to get sick."

"What about the shot?" Hope asked.

"Doc said it wasn't strong enough," Emily cried. "That's why he needed special blood."

"Your blood," Hope said with guilt on her face. "Doc gave Daddy your blood so he could fight the virus."

Emily nodded as tears streamed down her face.

"It killed the virus," Emily continued to sob. "But now Daddy is in a coma like I was before, and we don't know if he'll wake up."

Emily felt her mask entirely fall away as she finished. Telling her kids the story of what was going on was more than she could take.

"I'll take you to see him," Emily cried. "Doc is going to take him off the pain medication that's making him sleep in a few days. I want him to have a chance to hear you guys."

"Like you could hear us when you were in a coma," Hope said slowly.

"Yes," Emily nodded.

"Why didn't you want us to see him until he woke up before?" Steven asked, confused.

"Because," Emily sobbed. "I wanted you to remember him like he was, just in case."

"So you weren't just going to visit," Hope said slowly. "You were trying to save him."

Emily nodded as she wiped the tears from her face.

"I'm sorry," Emily said, looking between them.

"No, I'm sorry," Hope said with tears as she hugged Emily. "I shouldn't have gotten mad at you."

"You didn't know," Emily assured her as she hugged Hope with one arm and Steven with the other.

"We'll wait," Steven said softly.

"We'll wait," Hope repeated.

"Are you guys hungry?" Emily asked as they slowly released the hug.

"Not really," Steven said, looking at Hope, who agreed.

Emily looked at them and could see the exhaustion in their eyes. She doubted that either of them had slept the night before.

"Maybe we should go to bed early tonight?" Emily said to them.

Both kids looked at each other with a look of panic. Emily had been a mom long enough to recognize it.

"You guys can sleep in my room if you want," Emily offered.

"Okay," Hope said, and Steven quickly agreed.

"You guys get dressed, and I'll meet you there.

Emily walked out of the room and watched as Steven ran down the hall to his room. She made her way into the bedroom and quickly fixed the bed from the night before. As soon as she was done, Marley jumped on the bed and lay at the bottom. He seemed to understand what the plan was and where he would fit.

Emily went to the bathroom and quickly changed into her pajamas. Hope and Steven were already in bed when she came back out.

"Did you brush your teeth?" Emily asked as she walked closer to the bed to join them.

"Yes," both Hope and Steven nodded.

"Alright," Emily said, carefully eyeing them both.

Emily pulled the blankets over herself as she lay back on the bed.

"You having a slumber party without me?" Dillon's voice came from the doorway.

"The inn is full," Emily said to him, motioning to the bed.

"That's alright," Dillon said as he put his blanket and pillow on the floor. "I can make this work."

"You don't have to watch me anymore," Emily said, confused.

"I know," Dillon said as he sat down.

"Then why are you sleeping on the floor?" Steven asked, sitting up.

"It can't be comfortable," Hope added.

"I've slept on worse," Dillon said as he patted the floor. "Besides, until Shawn comes home, it's my job to keep you safe."

"I think we're safe in the house," Emily laughed.

"Yeah, but I'm not going to risk being wrong and him putting me in the hospital," Dillon sighed as he put his pillow behind his head.

"Have it your way," Emily said, realizing nothing she could say would get him to move. "Let's lie back down."

Hope and Steven slunk back into the bed beside her. Emily listened and in a few minutes, each of their breathing changed, and she knew that they were asleep. Soon after, Marley began to snore from the end of the bed, and Dillon from the hallway. Emily lay in the dark for a long time, listening to her family's sleep sounds.

She tried to close her eyes several times but was always forced to open them again. Each time she saw the scene on the wall again. The look on Shawn's face. The blood spilled from his chest. She had told the kids everything that had happened except for one thing. She hadn't said to them that it was her fault.

Chapter 11

The following day, Emily was awoken by a loud crashing sound. She sat straight in the bed with the kids as Marley began to growl.

"What the fuck is that?!" Dillon yelled as he jumped up in the hallway.

"What's going on out there?" Emily asked into the walkie as she jumped out of bed and threw on some clothes.

"They are trying to ram the gate!" Sarah's panicked voice came back.

"We'll get to the cellar," Hope said in a shaky voice.

Emily watched as she and Steven made their way out of the room.

"Make sure they get there and then find me," Emily said to Dillon before taking off down the stairs with Marley.

"I will," Dillon called down after her.

Emily made her way outside as the loud crashing sound happened once more. Everyone was on the street, and panic could be seen in their eyes. Emily took off running with Marley beside her. She glanced at the clinic as she went, where Shawn still lay unconscious. Her blood began to boil while she continued.

"What are they using?!" Emily asked as she ran in. "A fucking tank?!"

"Yeah," Sarah replied, pointing to a monitor.

"It doesn't even look to be scratching it," Will said, walking up beside her. "Just making one hell of a racket."

"What's the point?" Emily asked them all, frustrated.

"To scare us," Dillon said, walking in. "Did you not see everyone out there? They are all terrified."

"My guys stayed between the plates," Will said, looking at her. "But the others…."

"Are too scared," Emily finished for him.

Everyone looked at Emily, and she could see the same fear building in their eyes. She had to show them that there was nothing to be afraid of. She made her way over to the control panel and pressed the button.

"Good morning to you, too," Emily said in her most chipper voice.

"There you are," Clint said, walking into view.

Emily breathed a sigh of relief as the tank stopped moving.

"There are easier ways to get my attention," Emily replied.

"Yeah, but this seemed like fun," Clint smiled. "The General wants to speak to you."

Emily didn't have time to say anything as The General walked into view of the camera. He was standing in the open for the first time.

"Of course," Emily said under her breath.

He knew they couldn't have anyone on the wall, and he was safe out there.

"Just wanted to check in and see how Shawn was doing," The General smiled at the camera. "I heard there was a nasty little accident the other day."

Emily felt her body begin to shake uncontrollably with rage. He knew it was no accident. He had told that sniper to aim for Shawn.

"Thought I would make another offer to spare you any more accidents," The General smiled. "I assume you put Shawn down but send out the others, and we'll leave you alone."

Emily's eyes opened wide at the realization. He thought Shawn had died. He didn't know that Shawn was still alive, unconscious, but alive.

"He's lost all his spies," Emily said to herself.

"We can't know that," Sam said, stepping forward.

"If he knew Shawn was still alive, he would be asking for him," Emily said, looking at Sam.

"She's right," Dillon added. "He can't get anyone in and has no one here to feed him information anymore."

"That's a small victory," Alec grinned.

"Can I assume your silence means you are getting them all together?" The General asked, turning their attention back to the monitor.

"Not exactly," Emily couldn't help but smile as she spoke. "We're actually discussing something else."

"This is the only deal," The General glared at the camera.

"I know," Emily nodded. "But to be honest, we are bored with this situation, so we discussed the best cake."

"Cake?!" The General replied, losing his temper.

"Yeah, cake," Emily almost laughed.

"You think this is a joke?" The General sneered.

"Believe me, I know it's not," Emily replied flatly.

"You have two people dead," The General sneered. "Maybe your daughter should be the next. Hope, right?"

Emily felt her anger return in full force as he said Hope's name.

"Oh, so I've got your attention now," The General said after a few minutes of silence. "So, the living get your attention, not those who just died."

Emily still didn't reply as her anger continued to build.

"He wants you to lose your temper," Dillon spoke up. "If you are angry, you'll make a mistake."

"Like I did on the wall," Emily heard herself say out loud.

Everyone in the COM building was quiet. She hadn't told them all she blamed herself. Some probably knew the day it happened, but none knew that she still carried that feeling. Emily couldn't look at them as she forced herself to calm down.

"I care about them all," Emily said to The General.

"Then give me what I want," The General said firmly. "Or next time, we'll do more than make a little noise."

"Go to hell," Emily said firmly.

"We'll give you some time to think about your decision," The General said casually. "But not too much."

"I don't need time," Emily said firmly.

"I insist," The General smiled. "We wouldn't want any more blood on your hands. Would we?"

Emily watched the monitor as the tank and everyone headed back up the logging road.

"Where are the dead?" Emily said, turning to Sarah.

"They pulled most of them away," Sarah explained.

"But that racket should have drawn them back," Emily pointed out.

"It did," Sarah continued. "But as they returned, the soldiers gathered them in trucks."

"They are stealing our guard dogs," Will sighed.

"He sees it as taking them back," Dillon said through gritted teeth. "He thinks the dead have one purpose on this earth, to serve him."

"Of course he does," Emily sighed.

"He still can't get through the gate," Will pointed out. "No matter how many dead servants he gathers."

"He wants her to open it for him," Dillon continued. "His only goal today was to try to scare everyone into making her do it."

"Then I'd better get out there," Emily said, turning back to the door.

"And say what?" Dillon gasped.

"The truth," Emily replied as she walked past him.

The main street was full of terrified people as she walked out. Emily stopped outside the door and watched as their eyes turned to her.

"Just a show," Emily said with all the confidence she could muster. "He just wanted to get us all rattled up."

"Did the outer gate hold?" Someone yelled up to her from the crowd.

"He didn't even dent it," Emily smiled. "He just wanted to make a bunch of noise to scare us."

Emily looked around at the faces and could tell that he had succeeded.

"We're too strong for him," Emily continued. "He planned to scare all of you to force me to open the gate."

"What will he do next?" someone asked.

"I don't know," Emily admitted. "I'm sure he has a plan, but he's not exactly sharing it. The only thing I know for sure is that I will not open that gate."

"Maybe we should give him Veronica and Chad?"

"We can't do that without opening the gate," Emily sighed. "I'm sure he has people waiting for that to happen so he can rush us and get inside."

"So, we're trapped?!"

"We're together and safe," Emily smiled. "We must continue living our lives and be ready as best we can."

Emily could see that everyone was calming down as she spoke. After so many of these speeches, she was starting to get the hang of it.

"I'm sure we all have a lot to do today," Emily said. "Let's not waste another minute of it because of that madman."

Everyone nodded and slowly began to fan out. Emily breathed a sigh of relief as she walked back into the COM building.

"Nicely done," Alec smiled at her.

"It comes with the job," Emily said with a shrug.

"I think we all need to address the remaining issue," Sarah said, stepping forward. "What did you mean by the mistake you made on the wall?"

Emily could not bring herself to meet Sarah's gaze.

"You know it wasn't your fault that Shawn was shot, right?" Sarah asked.

"It was my fault," Emily said, not looking at her. "I lost my temper, threatened to throw Veronica off the wall, and Shawn paid the price."

"He had planned to shoot Shawn before that," Dillon spoke up.

"That sniper was in place with the laced bullet and already had orders to shoot Shawn before you even reached the wall," Will added.

Emily could feel all eyes on her as they spoke.

"I know he was in place and had the bullet," she sighed. "But the order had to come after."

"No," Dillon said, shaking his head. "He would have done it regardless. The only thing that could have stopped him was if you had opened that gate."

"And even then, he probably would have done it for fun," Will added. "Crazy people don't take logic into consideration."

"He's right," Dillon nodded. "Shawn would have been shot no matter what you did. You saved him by not opening the gate."

"Saved him?" Emily said as tears began to build up in her eyes. "He's lying in a hospital bed right now!"

"He's alive," Sam said, stepping towards her.

Emily pulled away from him as he tried to place his hand on her shoulder.

"He's unconscious, and we don't know if he'll wake up," Emily sobbed.

"He has a chance," Alec said softly. "If you had opened that gate, he wouldn't even have that."

"Good for me," Emily said with sarcasm. "I give you a chance, but there's still a good likelihood you'll get killed because of me."

"Stop it!" Dillon yelled, causing her to jump.

Emily turned and looked at him for a moment. Anger was washing over him in waves, which was evident in the air around them.

"Giving us a chance is more than we ever got out there," Dillon said, his body shaking in rage. "If Shawn were awake, he would…." "But he's not!" Emily yelled back.

She didn't give Dillon time to respond as she stormed out of the building, slamming the door. Emily looked around and wiped the tears from her eyes.

"Mommy!" Hope yelled as she came running towards her.

Emily pulled herself together as she put her brave face on for the kids.

"You guys did good," Emily smiled at them.

"I can't wait until we don't have to hide there anymore," Steven sighed. "It's so hot down there."

"I know," Emily said as she pulled him close. "But it's the safest place."

"No, it's not," Hope said with a smile. "The safest place is with you."

Emily felt like that sweet comment plunged a knife into her heart. In all honesty, the kids were safer, far away from her.

"If she would stop running into danger," Steven said with a smile.

"Soon," Emily nodded. "I was just going to see Daddy. Do you guys want to come?"

Both kids nodded excitedly and took her hands. She knew she wasn't ready for this, but remembered her promise. She didn't want to put it off with everything so uncertain.

"I thought you'd be stopping by," Doc smiled at her as she walked in. "And with some extra visitors."

"How's daddy?" Hope asked, her joyful tone gone.

"Much better," Doc nodded. "I've taken him off most of the pain medication."

"Any change?" Emily asked, meeting his eyes.

"Not yet," Doc said, shaking his head. "But I wouldn't expect there would be."

"Will he be able to hear us?" Steven asked.

"Maybe," Doc smiled. "Doesn't hurt to talk to him just in case."

With that, Doc stepped aside, and Emily led the kids into Shawn's room. Emily closed the door and saw the hurt on both kids' faces. Shawn did look better today, but still didn't look like the man they knew. Emily wrapped her arms over their shoulders and tried her best to comfort them.

"Can I ..." Hope began looking up at her.

Emily nodded and let go of Hope. Hope made her way over to the bed and took Shawn's hand.

"Hi, Daddy," Hope said as tears began to roll down her face.

Steven pulled away from Emily and walked over to join Hope.

"I'm taking good care of them, Daddy," Steven said as he cried.

"We're taking good care of each other," Hope corrected him.

"We need you to get better soon," Steven spoke next.

"We miss you, Daddy," Hope said, squeezing his hand.

Emily felt her eyes lock on Shawn's face. She could have sworn she saw his eyes try to open.

"We love you," Both Hope and Steven said.

Emily locked her eyes on Shawn for any further sign that he was waking up.

"Mommy?" Hope said, pulling her gaze away from Shawn.

"Yeah," Emily said, shaking her head, thinking she must have imagined what she saw.

"We should go home now," Hope continued. "He won't be happy with us if we start ignoring our chores."

"Of course," Emily smiled at her. "Why don't you two run ahead with Marley, and I'll catch up."

Emily waited until the kids left and then walked over to Shawn. She took hold of his hand before sitting down in her chair.

"It's been an interesting morning," Emily said as she looked at Shawn. "He tried to ram the gate with a tank. I'm sorry if the noise bothered you."

Emily looked at Shawn almost as if waiting for him to reply. Shawn lay still, and no reply came.

"He's not asking for you anymore," Emily continued. "He thinks I put you down. He doesn't know us very well, does he?"

"He does not," Doc said, walking into the room.

Emily gave him a tight smile before returning her gaze to Shawn.

"You should go home," Doc said, looking at her. "I'll call if there is any change."

"I can't leave him," Emily replied, not looking away from Shawn.

"He said the same thing when you were here," Doc smiled. "But then he realized you would beat him if things fell apart around here."

"I don't know how to do it without him," Emily admitted as she began to cry.

"You're not," Doc assured her. "He's taught you everything you need to keep going until he's back on his feet. Just like you taught him to keep going when you were down."

Emily nodded as she wiped the tears from her face.

"Just focus on those kids," Doc continued. "You have to do both jobs for a little while."

"I'll come back tomorrow," Emily said as she stood and kissed Shawn on the forehead.

Emily forced herself to walk out of the room. She didn't dare to look back at him because she knew she wouldn't leave. To her surprise, Dillon was waiting for her in the lobby. His anger seemed gone, but he still didn't look happy.

"How is he?" Dillon asked.

"Better," Emily nodded. "He's off most of the medicine, and now we just have to wait and see."

"If you doubt he'll wake up, then he won't," Dillon said flatly.

Emily stood in silence as she didn't know what to say.

"It's not your fault," Dillon continued. "And I will keep reminding you of that until he wakes up to tell you himself."

Emily was surprised that she found comfort in his words. Dillon turned and held the door of the clinic open for her. Emily walked through it without saying a word. Dillon followed behind her as she made her way back to the house.

Inside, the kids were busy doing their chores and doing what Shawn normally would. Emily and Dillon jumped in to help them. It didn't take long before everything was done. The kids made their way upstairs to make presents for Shawn. Emily sat down on the couch and was surprised when Dillon joined her.

"You don't have to watch me all the time," Emily said with a tight smile. "It's okay for you to do your own thing."

"My thing is taking care of you and those kids until he's back on his feet," Dillon said flatly.

"You're not sleeping in the hall anymore," Emily said firmly. "You being sore isn't going to allow you to protect anyone."

"I don't want to leave you alone," Dillon replied. "Defenseless."

"I was taking care of myself long before you or Shawn came along," Emily said with another smile.

Dillon nodded as he thought. Emily felt herself getting nervous as she waited for his reply.

"I'll move back to my room when the kids do," he said after several moments. "If they don't feel safe enough to sleep in their own beds, neither will I."

"Okay," Emily agreed.

She knew that getting him to agree to return to his room was an accomplishment, and she wasn't going to push it any further. Dillon kept her in sight the rest of the day. He helped her make dinner and look through all the presents the kids had made for Shawn. Emily gathered some extra blankets on the hallway floor as the kids announced they would sleep with her again tonight.

Emily got the kids into bed and crawled beside them as they quickly fell asleep. She looked at the doorway and could see Dillon sitting in the dark.

"What are you afraid is going to happen?" Emily asked.

"The way you were talking, you blame yourself and don't think you can live without him," Dillon said flatly.

"So?" Emily asked. This was precisely how she felt, but it didn't explain why she now had a constant bodyguard.

"I've known people like that before," Dillon replied. "And all of them ended up taking their own lives. I'm here to force you to live until you know you can do it yourself."

Emily looked up at the ceiling in the dark. She had never expressed that the thought of suicide had crossed her mind, even if it was only for a fraction of a second. She thought she was putting on a brave face, but apparently, Dillon could see deeper into her than she thought.

Chapter 12

The weeks passed slowly, and the air began to turn cool around them. Shawn's injuries were healed, according to Doc, but he still hadn't woken up. Emily visited him twice daily, once by herself and once with the kids. Dillon stopped by now and then but seemed uncomfortable each time.

Emily was doing better with the situation. Once she moved past the incident, the kids seemed to relax. They had both moved back to their rooms, and now it was just her and Marley in bed. Dillon had been true to his word and moved back to his room. Even though Emily knew that he came upstairs a couple of times a night and checked on all of them.

The General had continued to return every few days. Sometimes he put on a show by ramming the gate, and on others, he tried to plead with her. Emily decided to no longer give him the satisfaction of talking to him. She ignored him each time, and after a few hours, he would always leave. His antics didn't even faze the people inside anymore. Most of them continued like he wasn't even there. The kids continued to go to the cellar, just in case. But other than that, nothing was disturbed by him anymore.

Emily was on her way to pay her regular morning visit to Shawn. The kids were at school, and she would return with them later that day. Emily opened the door to the clinic as Marley followed her in.

"How is he today?" Emily asked as she walked in.

"His toxin levels continue to drop," Doc smiled.

"That's a good sign," Emily nodded.

She knew from personal experience that it would take time for the levels to be low enough for him to wake. Emily walked towards Shawn's door and reached for the handle. She was stopped as explosions seemed to be happening outside.

"What the hell?!" Emily yelled as she turned and ran back out of the clinic with Doc behind her.

Emily looked around and could see worried people running through the street. Just then, another explosion happened just above her. Emily looked up to see it in the sky.

"The General is back," Will said, running towards her.

"Is anyone hurt?" Emily asked.

"No," Will said, shaking his head. "All the explosions are happening way up there, and there is no debris falling that could hurt anyone."

"The kids are in the cellar," Jacob said as he joined them.

"And he's demanding to talk to you," Sarah said as she ran up.

"Tell everyone to get inside until this is over," Emily said to all of them. "It's just another show to get us all worked up."

"Are you going to talk to him?" Sarah asked.

"No," Emily said, shaking her head. "I've got more important things to do."

Emily made her way through the streets, looking for Dillon. He had been with The General for years and might know something about this new tactic. It didn't take her long to find him standing in front of the wall, looking up.

"This is new," Emily said as she walked toward him.

"I don't understand why he would waste them," Dillon said, looking back at her.

"He's just trying to scare us again," Emily replied.

"I don't think so," Dillon said, shaking his head. "I think this is like the bullet. It may be more than it seems."

Emily looked up as another explosion went off.

"Even if it is the virus, everyone here is immune to the airborne version," Emily said as the explosions continued.

"That's why I don't understand," Dillon said.

Emily and Dillon stood together for several minutes until the explosions stopped.

"Finally," Emily sighed as she felt herself relax.

"Emily!" Sarah's voice rang out from the COM building. "You should see this!"

Emily glanced at Dillon before they both took off running. They ran inside to see everyone gathered around the monitor.

"I'm tired of waiting," The General sneered through the monitor. "This present is sure to affect more than one person."

Emily stood in silence, watching the monitor as The General left.

"What present?" Joe said, looking back at Emily. "Is he talking about the explosions?"

"The virus would have to be airborne then," Doc said. "And everyone here is immune to that."

"It's probably just to get us worked up," Emily said calmly.

"I don't think so," Dillon said beside her. "I don't know the plan with this, but I promise you, he's got one."

Emily felt her stomach knot up as he finished. Dillon knew The General better than anyone, and she knew him to be right about his motives.

"Let's shut down everything nonessential for today," Emily said, looking back at the others. "No one is to be alone, and if anyone starts to feel off, they report to Doc immediately."

"This may cause some panic," Sam said with worry.

"It's just a precaution," Emily assured him. "We don't want to risk anyone."

Sarah nodded and quickly announced the speakers.

"You should get home," Dillon said, turning towards her. "The kids will be there soon, and you don't want them sitting there alone."

"You're right," Emily nodded as she walked towards the door.

Emily made her way up the street with Marley and reached the house simultaneously with the kids.

"What happened?" Hope asked, worried.

"Just The General," Emily smiled at her.

"What did he do?" Steven asked.

"Same as usual. He made a bunch of noise and left."

Emily didn't want them to worry, so she kept the conversation light.

"Then why are we shutting down?" Hope asked.

Hope knew her too well. She knew that Emily kept everything running except in emergencies.

"It really scared everyone," Emily admitted. "I thought it best to give them a day to steady their nerves."

Emily watched Hope closely and breathed a sigh of relief when Hope accepted her explanation. They all headed inside without another word. The kids set off to do various things while Emily went to the study with Marley. She had just sat at the desk when the walkie came to life.

"Found something strange on the south side," Will's voice rang out.

"Strange?" Emily replied.

"I'll bring it to you," Will said, and the walkie went dead.

What could he have found that he didn't want to say over the walkie? Emily waited nervously in her chair for Will to arrive. A few minutes later, the front door opened, and Will walked into her office.

"What is it?" Emily asked as he shut the door.

Will walked over and laid it on her desk. Emily couldn't speak as she reached and picked up the cell phone.

"The two we have are locked up," Emily said, looking at him.

"I radioed Alec on the way here," Will said. "He confirms that they are both still there."

"Did you tell him you found this?" Emily asked.

"No, didn't want to cause a panic," Will replied.

"This means that either someone here is still trying to help them, or they found a way in," Emily sighed.

"He's been trying to get in for weeks," Will replied. "If he could, he would have overrun us by now."

"So, we still have a traitor inside the wall," Emily sighed.

"That was not there this morning when I did a sweep," Will said.

"Who was guarding where this was found?" Emily asked with her stomach in a knot.

"Dillon," Will replied with hurt in his eyes.

"There's no way he would do this," Emily gasped. "After everything The General did to him…."

"After everything done to him, we all just accepted that he was good at heart and forgave him," Will interrupted. "I don't want to believe it, but we must accept that it is possible to be true."

"No," Emily said, shaking her head. "There has to be another explanation."

"I'm sure there is," Will sighed. "I just think we should be careful."

"Put this in the box with the others," Emily said, handing the phone back to him. "This stays between you and me."

"Yes, ma'am," Will said as he took the phone and left.

Emily collapsed back into her chair and put her head in her hands. Anyone could have dropped that phone there, and she refused to believe it could be Dillon. The General wanted her dead, and Dillon had more than enough opportunities to kill her. He had spent weeks doing everything he could to ensure she stayed alive.

"You look worried," Dillon said as he walked into the study.

Emily jumped as she looked up at him.

"Jumpy?" Dillon laughed.

"Just got a lot on my mind," Emily admitted.

"I'm here if you want to talk," Dillon said as he sat down.

Emily knew she couldn't tell him about the phone without mentioning that he was their prime suspect. She would tell him everything as soon as she could find the responsible person. "Just wish we could catch a break for five minutes," Emily sighed as she sat back.

"It can't be like this forever," Dillon assured her.

"You're right," Emily admitted.

She knew they would either end The General or The General would end them. Either way, this would end.

"The kids were hungry, so I fed them a little bit ago," Dillon said, pulling her back into the conversation. "I left the sandwich stuff out if you're still hungry."

"I'm not right now, but thank you," Emily replied.

"You got a lot to do in here?" Dillon asked, looking around.

"Just make sure everyone knows what they're supposed to do," Emily smiled.

"So, yes," Dillon laughed. "I'll take care of dinner then and let you know when it's ready."

"I appreciate it," Emily grinned.

She knew that meant grilled cheese sandwiches, but she didn't complain. Emily waited until Dillon left before grabbing her walkie. She checked in with everyone and had them all organized a few hours later. She remained in her office until Hope appeared to bring her to dinner.

Emily ate dinner with the family, grilled cheese, just like she predicted. After dinner, the kids were exhausted and decided to head to bed early. Emily quickly tucked them each in before heading back downstairs.

"Cole?" Emily said as she reached the bottom of the stairs.

"Thought I would come personally and give you the evening report," Cole smiled at her.

Emily walked over and sat down on the couch with Cole.

"Everyone is doing much better this evening," Cole began. "They are all ready to return to work tomorrow. Only one person came to see Doc. They were feeling sick and had thrown up a few times. But it just turned out to be a parasite."

"Parasite?" Emily asked.

"She's pregnant," Cole laughed. "It will clear up in a few months."

"I've never heard it called a parasite before," Emily laughed.

It had been a while since she honestly laughed. It felt good, but at the same time, she felt guilty. How could she laugh when Shawn was still in the clinic?

"Don't go doing that now," Cole scolded her.

"What?" Emily said in surprise.

"Thinking you shouldn't smile because he's not up yet," Cole looked at her, knowing.

"I just feel a little guilty," Emily admitted. "But I know he would want me to smile."

"Damn straight!" Cole said, smacking his knee. "And that is my personal goal." "To make me smile?" Emily laughed.

"At least once a day," Cole nodded. "Until the big guy can get up and give you a real reason to smile.

Emily felt her cheeks blush as she playfully smacked Cole on the shoulder.

"I refuse to try to fill in that department," Cole laughed. "Wouldn't want to put the guy to shame or anything."

"Stop it," Emily laughed. "Or I'll tell him you said that."

"Tell him who said what?" Dillon asked, walking into the room.

"You don't want to know," Emily laughed.

"Well, I'd better get back home," Cole said, standing up. "I'll see you all in the morning."

Emily waved goodbye as Cole left, and Dillon took his place on the couch. Emily felt the smile disappear from her face as she looked at him. He was obviously worried and needed to talk.

"What's going on?" Emily asked.

"Something's going to happen," Dillon said slowly. "I can just feel that something is wrong."

"No one's getting sick," Emily explained. "We only have a report of one pregnancy and no other illness."

"What did Will find?" Dillon asked, catching her off guard.

She had forgotten that Will had made the announcement over the public channel. She had hoped to hide it from Dillon until she found out who had actually dropped the phone. But now she knew she had to tell him.

"One of the General's phones," Emily said slowly.

"Where?!" Dillon asked, his eyes wide in fear.

"Where were you on guard duty this morning?" Emily replied, looking at her hands.

"So, it looks like I dropped it," Dillon said, balling his fists.

"I don't think it was you," Emily quickly spoke. "That's why I didn't want to tell you until we found out who it was."

Dillon visibly relaxed a little at her words.

"Maybe that was the reason for the explosions," Emily continued. "Maybe we were so distracted we didn't notice something getting fired over the wall."

"The phone would have been shattered," Dillon said, shaking his head. "Part of the plan was definitely to get you to stop trusting me, but that doesn't explain how the phone got in here."

"We'll figure it out," Emily assured him. "Maybe we should just get some rest tonight."

"I'm going to wait a bit more," Dillon said, not moving. "Just to make sure."

"How about we watch a movie and then go to bed?" Emily offered. "I'll even let you pick."

Dillon nodded in agreement, made his way over to the DVDs, and put a disc in the player after a few minutes. Emily looked at him in shock as the title screen for Braveheart appeared.

"This is like three hours long," Emily gasped.

"But it's a great movie," Dillon smiled.

Emily knew that he had picked one of the longest movies he could find. He was expecting her to refuse and go to bed. Instead, she clicked play and got comfortable on the couch.

It was nearly midnight when the movie ended, and Emily struggled to stay awake. She waited as Dillon used the walkie and confirmed that everything was still quiet.

"We need to get some sleep," Emily said as she forced herself up off the couch.

"I think I'll sleep here," Dillon said, motioning to the couch. "Just in case."
"Fine," Emily said.

She was too tired to argue with him anymore tonight.

"I also want you to take these to you're room," Dillon said, reaching under the table.

Emily watched him, confused as he pulled out her and Hope's pistols and a box of ammo. She had no idea when he had put them there.

"What are these doing out?" Emily asked as she took the weapons.

"I checked them out earlier," Dillon explained. "Shawn had an emergency plan in place that allowed certain people to carry inside the wall during times of crisis."

"I'm not sure about this," Emily said slowly.

"At least for tonight?" Dillon pleaded. "I made sure only those Shawn had on the emergency plan had them."

"Just for tonight," Emily nodded. "But I'll keep Hope's in my room." "I figured," Dillon smiled.

"Now, you get some sleep," Emily said in her mom's voice.

"Yes, ma'am," Dillon yawned as he lay on the couch.

Emily went up the stairs and into her bedroom. She closed the door tonight since a loaded gun would be on her nightstand. She quickly dressed for bed and put her gun on the nightstand, and Hope's in the drawer. She ensured the volume on her walkie was turned up before climbing into bed.

As soon as she lay down, she was suddenly wide awake. She stared at where the walkie sat, waiting for someone to speak. It remained silent, but Emily's mind continued to race.

"I have to stop," Emily said as she forced herself to roll over and look away from the walkie.

Emily closed her eyes and lay still in the dark. After a few minutes, she grabbed Shawn's pillow and held it close to her chest. Though it had been weeks since he used it, it still smelled like him. She breathed deeply, finding the comfort she needed to finally fall asleep.

Chapter 13

"Honey, I'm home!" a loud voice ripped Emily from her dreamless sleep.

Emily immediately recognized the voice and turned to grab the pistol from her nightstand. Once she had it, she turned to point it at her intruder. Emily stared at Chad and Veronica, who were grinning in her doorway.

"Hope you don't mind me using your line," Veronica sneered. "It just seemed like fun."

"What the fuck are you doing?!" Emily yelled as she switched between aiming the gun at Chad and Veronica.

They were both holding their gun, pointed directly at her. Neither of them looked well. Their time in the cells wasn't kind to them. While Emily had ensured they were fed regularly, Chad and Veronica, most of the time, refused the meals. Now, she could see the result of their decision.

Veronica's arms were pencil-thin, and her eyes were dark and sunken. Her hair hung dull and lifeless around her face. Emily was surprised that she even had the strength to hold the gun. Chad was in slightly better condition, but not much. He was skinnier, too, and seemed weak on his feet. He was trying to hide it, but Emily could tell he was leaning on the door frame for support.

Emily wasn't sure what to do. Shawn had told her never to hesitate with her shots. However, she knew she could only shoot one of them before the other killed her.

"I thought no one was allowed to carry inside the wall," Chad glared at her.

"New rule," Emily replied.

She was trying her best to hide the panic in her voice.

"More like you do whatever the hell you want," Veronica growled. "Now be a good little bitch and tell us the code."

"Fuck off," Emily replied.

"Then maybe we should go see Hope, and then you'll be willing to talk," Chad said as he leaned up off the doorway.

"You stay the fuck away from her!" Emily yelled, causing him to stop.

She felt a pain in her heart at Chad's willingness to hurt Hope. Not for herself but for Hope. Hope still dreamed that maybe one day Chad would change and be the father Emily made him out to be in her storybook. Emily knew that Chad was a vile man, but this was even lower than she thought he could go.

"Then give us the code!" Veronica yelled, pulling Emily's attention back to her...

Emily tried to think of something fast. She couldn't let Chad hurt Hope, but she also couldn't give them the code. She could give them a fake one. One of them would have to leave to test, which may give her the needed opening.

"You promise you'll leave my kids alone?" Emily asked.

She knew they would be suspicious if she just blurted it out. Veronica glanced back at Chad as they both smiled.

"We're taking Steven," Chad said shortly. "But you can keep the mistake."

Emily felt her blood boil as he spoke about Hope. It really was an act that he put on about caring about her. She was tempted to shoot him right then. But she had to be smart about this.

"I have your word?" Emily asked.

"We promise," Veronica said, rolling her eyes. "Now give us the damn code!"

Emily opened her mouth but was unable to speak. She could see someone moving through the dark in the hall. It was too tall to be one of the kids.

"Dillon!" she thought to herself.

With Chad and Veronica's attention on her, he could sneak up behind them. She had to keep their eyes on her.

"Fine," Emily said as she lowered the gun slowly.

"Good girl," Veronica mused.

Emily could see both Veronica and Chad relax as she played defeated.

"It's eleven twenty-nine," Emily said, glancing up at them.

She said the first set of numbers that she could think of. Her mind was racing to find an explanation for why she would use that code.

"Really?" Chad said, surprised.

"What?" Veronica asked, glancing at him.

"It's my birthday," Chad said, surprised. "Why would you use my birthday?"

Emily contained her smile. She couldn't help but find it funny that Veronica did not even know Chad's birthday.

"No one would guess I would use it," Emily said flatly. "Not even you."

"Clever bitch," Veronica laughed. "By the way."

Emily looked up to see Veronica raising her gun once more. Emily knew that Veronica had no intentions of letting her live, but expected them to at least verify that the code was actually real first. Apparently, her explanation was more convincing than she thought, or Veronica was an idiot.

"We lied," Veronica said with a smile.

Emily held her breath as a shot rang out. She sat still and waited for the pain, but none came. She focused on Veronica and Chad just as both fell to the floor. Behind where they once stood was Dillon, still holding a pistol up.

"Dillon," Emily said with relief.

"Couldn't risk two shots," Dillon explained, walking into the room. "I had to get them lined up just right. Are you alright?"

"I'm fine," Emily said, looking down at herself.

She half expected to find a bullet hole in her somewhere, but neither of them had a chance to pull the trigger.

"Mommy!" Hope and Steven's voices rang out.

"Shit," Emily said as she jumped out of bed and ran towards the door.

Emily glanced down at Veronica and Chad's bodies as she rushed over them. There had only been one shot, but a bullet hole was in each of their heads. Dillon had lined them up perfectly. This probably would have scared her in an ordinary world, but she couldn't help but be grateful.

"We heard a shot!" Hope exclaimed as Emily met the kids and Marley just outside the door.

"Everything's okay," Emily assured them.

She tried her best to be calm despite everything that had just happened.

"What happened?" Steven asked with a shaky voice.

"Someone broke in, but Dillon stopped them," Emily explained.

She wasn't sure they could handle the truth about who had just died in their house. She didn't want to lie to them and decided to be vague. Marley walked past her into the bedroom. Emily heard him let out a low growl before he returned and sat beside her.

"Who?" Hope asked as she and Steven pushed past Emily.

"Wait!" Emily said as she tried to stop both of them.

They both managed to get into the room before she could get a grip on them. Emily followed them in. They both stopped and looked down at Chad and Veronica's bodies.

"Chad and Veronica?" Hope said, looking back at her.

Emily expected to see tears in her eyes, but they were cold and uncaring. She thought Hope was trying to be brave and decided to explain what had happened.

"Dillon had to, or they would have killed me," Emily explained.

"They're finally gone," Steven said with the sound of relief in his voice.

It was not exactly the reaction that Emily expected from either of them. She could understand Hope being able to be detached to an extent, but Steven, she was not ready for. Emily knew that Steven had suffered significantly at their hands, but they were his parents. They had raised him for years before finding Sanctuary.

"Thank you, Dillon," Steven said, wrapping his arms around Dillon.

Dillon was surprised for a moment, unsure of what to do. He wrapped one arm around Steven and looked at Emily, confused.

"Hope," Emily asked, pulling Hope's face to look at her.

"I'm okay," Hope assured her. "It's not like with Mrs. June. I don't feel anything for them."

Emily couldn't help but worry about Hope as she spoke. She seemed so cold about the whole situation. Emily felt more remorse, though not much, for the two people who were now dead.

"Maybe we should all go downstairs," Dillon said, looking just as concerned as Emily. "I'll radio and get them taken out of here." "Yeah," Emily nodded. "Let's...."

Emily stopped, and they all turned to look towards the window. Screams erupted in the streets and sounded like a war was occurring. "What the hell is going on out there?!" Emily yelled on the walkie as Dillon ran towards the window.

"They just turned," Sarah replied in a panic.

"There's dead out there," Dillon said, walking back towards her.

"In the nightstand," Emily said to Dillon as she pulled the kids close.

Dillon walked over to the nightstand and pulled out Hope's gun.

"I have to go help them," Emily said to Hope and Steven. "I need you guys to go to Hope's room and stay there. You don't open the door for anyone but me."

"But what if the dead come in?" Hope asked, sounding frightened.

"Then you know what to do," Emily said as she took the gun from Dillon and handed it to Hope.

"But daddy said I'm not supposed to use it without him," Hope said, looking back at her.

"I need you guys to protect each other," Emily said firmly. "Can you do that?"

Hope and Steven nodded before taking each other's hands and going to Hope's room. "You go with them," Emily said to Marley.

Marley sprinted to get into the room before the door closed.

"Let's go," Emily said, turning and heading towards the stairs.

"I can't," Dillon said, not moving from where he stood.

"What do you mean you can't?" Emily said as she turned back to him. "They need help!"

"I haven't shot anyone since I came here," Dillon said, looking at the gun he had placed on the dresser.

Emily followed his gaze to the gun. She hadn't even realized that he had set it down.

"You had to," Emily said as she walked toward him. "They would have killed the kids and me if you hadn't."

"I know," Dillon said softly. "But now it's two more names I need to add to the memorial. Two more lives that I ended."

"Do you regret what you did?" Emily asked, causing him to look at her with hurt in his eyes.

"No," Dillon replied. "I'd reshoot them to save you all."

"Do you regret the others?" Emily asked, referring to the names on the memorial.

"Of course," Dillon said with a slight hint of anger.

"Their bodies will be burned, and the world will be better off forgetting they ever existed," Emily said as she motioned to Chad and Veronica. "They don't deserve to be remembered or for their deaths to weigh on your conscious."

"I just…" Dillon was interrupted as both of their eyes were pulled back to the window. The screams outside were getting louder, and Emily couldn't help the panic rising inside her.

"Staying up here and feeling sorry for yourself will let people die!" Emily yelled, pointing to the window. "Innocent people that you could have saved. Those are names that will haunt you."

The screams grew louder, and Emily could see the change in Dillon's eyes. He grabbed his gun off the dresser and nodded to her.

"Let's go," Dillon said as he began to walk forward.

Emily turned and ran down the stairs with Dillon right behind her. She opened the front door and froze for just a moment at the sight of what was happening. There were dead in the streets, but the zombies did not get in. Emily stood still as she looked at the faces with milky white eyes.

"Thomas," Emily said, nearly crying as one of the zombies turned and began to walk towards them.

Thomas was one of their construction workers. He was covered in blood, but it didn't look like his own. Emily felt a hand on her shoulder and turned to look at Dillon with tears in her eyes. Dillon stepped in front of her and fired. Thomas's body fell to the ground on the street.

"They didn't let the zombies in," Emily said, looking at Thomas.

"The explosions," Dillon nodded. "He found a way to turn people inside the wall."

"We have to stop them," Emily said as she straightened herself.

Dillon nodded and took off into the street. Emily followed Dillon as he ran towards the bakery, where Julia was pinned down.

"Emily!" Joe yelled, causing her eyes to look towards him.

Emily got her hand up just in time to catch the crowbar he threw to her. She was much better with this than she was with a gun. She tucked the weapon into her jeans and gripped the crowbar. She turned back to the bakery to see that Dillon had handled the zombie and was helping Julia to her feet.

"Help!" a voice called out.

Emily turned to see Bobby standing just in front of the store.

The other kids were running through the streets. Each had their buddies from Shawn's training and were making their way to safety. Emily knew that Bobby was alone. His buddies were locked inside her house. Emily quickly made her way to Bobby and stabbed the zombie with the crowbar, clawing at him. She couldn't bring herself to look at the person's face, knowing it would hurt her heart too much, and she had to be focused.

"Get to my house," Emily said after looking over Bobby and seeing he wasn't injured. "Hope and Steven are in her room."

Bobby nodded and took off running towards the house. Emily watched him as she put down another zombie, still not looking at their face. She turned her attention back to the street as the front door closed. Despite Emily telling her not to open the door for anyone else, she knew Hope would let him in.

Emily slowly worked her way through the street, killing three more zombies as she did. As she reached the gate, she found a group of the others, each looking exhausted.

"What happened?" Emily said, walking towards them.

"She fell asleep," Alec said with tears running down his face. "I thought she was having a nightmare, but when I tried to wake her...."

Emily gasped as her eyes grew wide with realization.

"I had to," Alec cried. "We promised each other if it ever happened...."

Emily dropped her crowbar and ran forward, wrapping her arms around Alec.

"I'm so sorry," Emily said softly as he cried.

"I thought she was fine," Alec continued. "Doc said it was just morning sickness."

Emily's heart broke as she squeezed him tighter. Samara had been the one who was pregnant.

"It looks like something happened to them when they fell asleep," Will said beside her.

"Only certain people were affected, but they tended to bite whoever was lying next to them and then..." Sam said, looking out to the street.

Emily let go of Alec and turned her attention back to Sanctuary. The main street was drenched in blood, and bodies were scattered throughout. Blood was shed inside the walls for the first time since she came here.

"There are more in the houses and apartments," Will said, following her gaze. "We will gather them all and make arrangements."

"There are two bodies in my room," Emily said as her anger began to boil. "Just burn them."

"Who?" Will asked, looking down at her.

"Chad and Veronica," Emily said, not looking back at him.

"How the hell did they get out?" Will said, looking at the others.

"Or make it through town without anyone seeing?" Sam added.

"They waited until this started," Emily said slowly. "Until we were at our weakest."

"Still, someone had to let them out," Sam said.

"I'll find out who, and when I do, they will burn too," Emily said as she walked away from them.

None of them tried to stop her as she walked up the street. Her heart broke with each dead face she looked at, each loved one crying over a body. She had promised to keep them safe, and now they were lying dead in the street.

"Emily," Doc said as he walked out of the clinic.

"Any survivors?" Emily asked, looking at him.

"We have twelve that were bitten," he said slowly. "I have given them the antidote and moved them to quarantine."

Emily nodded and continued her way up the street. She instructed all children to be sent to her house while the adults handled what had happened. Shawn had trained the kids well, as none of them were among the dead or injured.

Emily worked with the rest of the adults through the night, clearing away the dead. Doc insisted they give him the next day to figure out what had caused them to turn. Emily agreed, wanting to ensure that The General could never do this to them again. Emily walked with Alec while carrying his wife to the clinic with the rest of the dead.

"I'm so sorry," Emily repeated as they walked back out.

Alec was a strong man, but right now, he looked like the slightest touch could break him.

"We have to end this," Alec said, looking at her slowly. "We can't lose anyone else." "I agree," Emily nodded.

"We have the count," Dillon said, walking towards her with Will.

Emily braced herself and nodded for him to continue.

"Twenty-two were killed in the initial fight," Dillon said slowly. "Another four have died in quarantine."

"Will the others recover?" Emily asked.

"Doc says it's too soon to tell," Will answered.

"Cole says he thinks it's working like it did before," Dillon spoke up.

"Cole was bitten?!" Emily said in shock.

She had just seen Cole, and he had been saying his primary mission was to make her smile every day. It hadn't even occurred to her that she had not seen him during the fight.

"Yes," Dillon nodded. "He said he thinks the shot is working like last time."

"It is," Doc said, running towards them. "The remaining eight have fallen asleep but still have no fever. They will be awake in a few hours, but I believe they will all be fine." Emily breathed a sigh of relief.

"Emily?" Dillon said, pulling her attention back to them.

"He wanted to prove that the wall can't protect us from everything," Emily said slowly.

Everyone nodded in agreement, not sure where she was going with this.

"Now it's time to show him he fucked with the wrong town," Emily said firmly.

Chapter 14

Emily did her best to hold her head high over the next few days. The cemetery had been prepared to bury all of their dead. The remaining eight that were bitten all made a full recovery. Cole came to see her as soon as he was released, but he even found it challenging to find a reason to smile.

Emily made her way to the clinic, hoping that Doc had finished his examination of the dead and they would finally be able to put them at rest. Marley walked beside her as she opened the door and walked inside. She found Doc in his office. He looked exhausted.

"Find anything?" Emily asked as she walked in.

"I know what caused it," Doc said, rubbing his eyes. "They all suffered a brain hemorrhage as soon as they fell asleep."

"How?" Emily asked, trying to hide her frustration.

"It has something to do with this chemical," Doc said, motioning to a paper on his desk. "But I've never seen it before, and I can't find anything about it."

"Probably something he had the scientists cook up," Emily said, looking over his shoulder.

"That doesn't stop them from doing it again," Doc sighed. "I don't know how to protect everyone from it."

"We'll figure it out," Emily assured him. "But for now, we need to lay them to rest."

"Of course," Doc nodded as he looked at her. "I'll inform everyone that they are ready. What do you want to do with Chad and Veronica?"

"I'll handle them after," Emily said coldly. "They don't get a grave."

"But we can't go outside, and burning them inside the walls is just...." Doc began.

"Remember the fire we started to get the bikers in?" Emily asked.

"Of course," Doc nodded.

"We'll just toss them over, pour the kerosene, and let them burn," Emily said. "Then, if The General wants his daughter, what's left will be outside waiting for him."

Doc nodded as he stood up. She knew that her plan was cold, but she didn't care. Doc seemed to understand that this was not the time to try to get her to be kind.

"I'll see you at the funeral," Emily said as she turned and left.

It wasn't long before the dead were safely in their coffins, lined up in front of the clinic. Emily walked over to join the crowd forming to put them all to rest. As each coffin was lifted, she stood silent with Hope, Steven, and Marley. Emily led the rest of the town behind the line of caskets to the graves.

Father Nathan gave a speech to each of the dead. Emily couldn't help but notice the bite he was covering on his hand. He had been one of the lucky ones who had survived quarantine. As he finished, he nodded to Emily. She motioned for the kids to stay with Julia as she walked up to join him.

"I know we all lost people we love, and the families will never be the same," Emily said, looking out at everyone. "The enemy found a way to attack us in our homes, which I will never forgive myself for."

Emily's eyes met with Alec's. He was crying openly as he held onto his daughters. Her heart broke for them, and she struggled to find the words. Alec looked back at her, and Emily saw something flash in his eyes. It wasn't pain or hurt but pure rage.

"But that's what he wants," Emily heard herself say. "He wants us to fall apart at our loss and give in to his demands. These people were here because they believed Sanctuary could provide our children and us with a brighter future. It is our job to make sure that belief becomes a reality."

Alec nodded, and Emily could see that the tears on his face were no longer running.

"He will be back," Emily continued. "This time to take more of our lives. But we will be ready for him. We are done hiding, and now it is time to fight back and protect what is ours."

Everyone in the crowd nodded, a few having to wipe the tears from their face.

"Then we'd better get busy," Alec said loudly as he set his kids down and took their hands.

Emily nodded in agreement and walked toward him. She waited as each family said their final goodbyes and was the last to leave the cemetery. Emily stepped back through the gate with Marley and was surprised to see the council waiting for her.

"We need more training programs for the adults," Alec said, stepping forward. "The fact that the kids were better prepared than us can't happen again."

"I agree," Emily nodded.

"If it's okay with you, I would like to have Will and Dillon do the training," Alec continued. "They helped with the kids and have a greater understanding of war than the rest of us."

"If they are willing, it is fine with me," Emily said, looking toward Will and Dillon.

"We'll set it up immediately," Will nodded in agreement. Dillon nodded as well but did not speak.

"I can't know for certain if they will work," Doc spoke next. "But we have a large supply of gas masks. I think one should be issued to everyone."

"It has to be better than nothing," Emily agreed.

"They would only need to wear them if the rockets begin to explode again," Doc continued.

"We'll get them handed out today," Jessica nodded.

"I'll make an announcement, so everyone knows what's going on," Sarah added.

"I know we have much more to do," Emily sighed. "But I have something I need to take care of."

"Time to take out the trash?" Dillon asked.

"Yeah," Emily nodded. "I don't even want their corpses in here."

"We'll get them," Dillon said as he turned towards the clinic with Will.

"I already put the kerosene on the wall," Cole said.

Emily looked at Doc. The only way for them all to know what she was planning was if he had told them. She had planned to do it alone, not wanting anyone else to deal with it.

"We want to help," Sam said beside her. "We're all in this together."

Emily nodded, and her expression softened towards Doc. He had only told them to help her, and she couldn't bring herself to stay mad about it.

Will and Dillon returned, each with a body draped over their shoulder in a white sheet. Emily led them up the wall and watched as each body was tossed over. Even as high up as they were, the bones breaking as they hit the ground could still be heard. Each of them was careful to keep low and not give any snipers a clear shot. Cole carefully poured over a few containers of kerosene. When he finished, he nodded to Emily.

"You ready?" Dylan asked as he handed her a jar with a rag and a lighter.

Emily took them from him and steadied herself. She flicked the lighter and carefully lit the cloth. She glanced down to ensure her aim as she dropped the bottle. She watched as the bottle hit the ground, and the bodies below were engulfed in flames.

"If they are still watching, he'll know that someone just got thrown over," Sam said as she sat down.

"I know," Emily agreed. "We need to get ready."

Everyone carefully made their way back off the wall. Emily breathed a sigh of relief, knowing they were all safer on the ground. She was left alone with Marley as everyone broke off to begin making preparations. Emily glanced at the wall and saw the black smoke rising from outside. The General was sure to see it even if the snipers weren't still watching.

"Let's go," Emily said to Marley as she made her way back up the street.

Emily paused while Sarah announced the gas masks. Emily expected to be swarmed with questions and concerns, but everyone nodded and continued. She was trying to decide what she should do.

Hope and Steven would stay with Bobby for the rest of the day. They had made sure to stay with him ever since the attack. They wanted their buddy group to be together as much as possible. Julia insisted that she didn't mind and was happy to have them all with her.

"Emily," Doc's voice came over the walkie.

"Go ahead," Emily responded.

"He's awake," Doc said quickly.

Emily felt like her heart had frozen in her chest. She could not move for a moment as Doc's words sank in.

"Emily," Doc said again into the walkie.

Emily didn't respond as she turned and ran to the clinic. Emily threw open the door with Marley right behind her. Doc was nowhere to be seen, so she quickly made her way to Shawn's room. Emily burst threw the door and froze again when Shawn looked at her.

"There you are, beautiful," Shawn smiled.

Emily said nothing as she closed the distance between them and wrapped her arms around his neck. She felt the tears run down her face as Shawn hugged her. Doc smiled at them and quietly made his way out of the room.

"Did you miss me?" Shawn said softly into her hair.

"I thought…" Emily choked as she tried to speak.

"From what Doc says, you made sure I was going to make it," Shawn said, kissing her head.

Shawn pulled Emily slowly onto the bed so that she was lying on his chest while he held her. Neither of them said anything for a long time and just lay together.

"What are you thinking?" Shawn said, breaking the silence.

"That I can't believe you're awake," Emily said softly.

"With all the naps you've taken over the years, I think I'm allowed one," Shawn smiled.

"I'm sorry," Emily said, lifting herself.

"For wanting me to wake up?" Shawn half laughed.

"No," Emily said seriously. "I'm sorry that you got shot. If I hadn't lost my temper, then…."

"No," Shawn cut her off. "This wasn't your fault."

Emily began to cry again as she looked at him. Shawn brought his hand up to softly caress her face.

"What did I miss?" Shawn asked her.

"A lot," Emily replied.

She knew Shawn would want to know what happened in Sanctuary, but didn't want to tell him just yet.

"I can see that in your eyes," Shawn replied. "I've never seen you look so broken."

Emily looked away, trying to find her strength again.

"Is it the kids?" Shawn asked, concerned.

"They're fine," Emily assured him. "They've been through a lot, but they're fine."

Shawn nodded but looked at her, waiting for her to continue.

"We just need to focus on you getting better," Emily said with a fake smile. "The rest of it can wait."

"I feel fine," Shawn insisted. "You can either tell me, or I will ask someone else."

"I…" Emily said, looking at him with both hurt and shock.

"Doesn't feel so good when you are trying to protect someone, and they refuse to wait, does it?" Shawn said with a smirk. "That's not fair," Emily pouted.

"Fair or not, I still want to know," Shawn said, taking her hand.

"Fine," Emily sighed. "The General has continued to come back every few days. He keeps making the same demands and thinks you are dead."

"That's all?" Shawn asked her.

The look in his eyes told her he knew she was holding back. Shawn wasn't going to accept this little bit of an explanation.

"I told him to go to hell, and he decided to move up from scare tactics," Emily sighed. "They fired some rockets over the wall, and they exploded in the air. We thought it was just another scare tactic until…."

"Until what?" Shawn asked, encouraging her to continue.

"Apparently, someone who had a phone during the explosions helped Chad and Veronica escape their cells."

"Any clues as to who?" Shawn asked.

"No," Emily said, shaking her head. "Will found the phone by the wall, where Dillon had been standing guard before the explosions."

"Set up," Shawn said firmly.

"We know," Emily nodded.

"So, explosions in the sky, and Chad and Veronica escaped," Shawn said.

"Not exactly," Emily admitted. "We didn't know they were out until late that night when they burst into our bedroom," Emily explained.

"What!?" Shawn said, shaking with anger.

"They demanded the gate code while holding me at gunpoint," Emily continued. "I was armed but knew if I fired at one, the other would kill me."

"I'm going to kill him," Shawn said in almost a growl.

"He's dead," Emily said. "Dillon heard them come in and shot them from behind before they could do anything."

Shawn accepted what she said, but she couldn't help but think he looked disappointed.

He had wanted to kill Chad since he pushed her down the wall.

"How are the kids holding up?" Shawn asked.

"They're fine," Emily assured him. "They both were kind of numb to it. Steven even seemed relieved that they were gone."

Shawn nodded but didn't say anything. Emily thought she could stop there and not tell him about the people who had died. She knew he wouldn't stay in the clinic and would find out as soon as he left.

"I didn't have much time to help them through it before it happened," Emily said slowly.

"What?" Shawn asked forcefully.

"The rockets," Emily began. "They released a chemical that caused some people to have a brain aneurysm when they fell asleep."

Shawn's face couldn't hide the shock he was feeling.

"They turned, and several people were bitten," Emily continued.

"How many did we lose?" Shawn asked her, lifting her chin to look at him.

"Twenty-six," Emily answered. "Alec's wife was among them. They had just found out she was pregnant. Eight others were bitten, but they were able to be saved."

"Holy shit," Shawn sighed as he ran his hands over his face.

"We buried them today and burned Chad and Veronica outside the wall," Emily finished. "You went out!" Shawn said, angry.

"No," Emily assured him. "Will and Dillon threw them over, and we lit them from above. We were careful not to give the snipers a shot."

Shawn nodded but still didn't speak.

"Dillon and Will are setting up a training plan for the adults," Emily explained. "The adults were upset that the kids were more prepared than they were."

"All of the kids were okay?" Shawn asked.

"Yes," Emily nodded. "They found their buddies and got to a safe place, just like you taught them. Bobby, Hope, and Steven held up in her room."

"Good," Shawn said, nodding.

"Hope was a little nervous about having her gun without you there, but she did good," Emily smiled at him.

"Is that everything?" Shawn asked her, raising his eyebrow.

"We're giving everyone gas masks in case they try the rocket thing again," Emily said. "But that's everything."

"Good," Shawn said, pulling her closer.

Emily lay her head back on his chest and closed her eyes.

"Emily," Shawn said as he ran his hand over her hair.

"Yeah," Emily replied.

"None of it was your fault," Shawn said. "Not me getting shot or what happened to those people."

Emily felt the tears well up in her eyes as he spoke. Hearing him say the words made the guilt she had carried since he was shot melt away. She didn't say anything but nodded as she snuggled closer to Shawn. His bullet wound had healed, but she could see the scar. She reached up and ran her fingers over it. Shawn gently took her hand and kissed her fingers.

"How are we doing?" Doc asked as he walked back into the room.

"Ready to get out of here," Shawn said, sitting up.

Emily sat up as well and took his hand.

"I don't want you alone for the rest of the day," Doc looked at him sternly. "And you have to eat and rest."

"I'll make sure of it," Emily smiled at Shawn.

"Then you guys should be good to go," Doc nodded. "You have quite the crowd waiting for you out there.

Emily stood up off the bed and waited while Shawn got dressed. Once he was ready, he took Emily's hand and led her out of the room. Marley jumped on him as soon as they walked out, excited to see Shawn again.

"Good boy," Shawn said as he petted Marley.

Emily laughed, watching the two of them. Marley finally got off Shawn, and Shawn took her hand once more. As he opened the door to the clinic, Emily saw the crowd that Doc said was waiting for them. Dillon stayed towards the front and immediately pulled Shawn into a hug. Emily stepped back and let them have their moment.

"You can't do that again," Dillon said as they pulled apart. "She is too much of a handful for me."

"That's because she needs a man," Shawn teased.

"Daddy!" Hope and Steven yelled as they came bursting through the crowd.

Shawn kneeled, allowing them to crash into his open arms.

"I missed you guys," Shawn said, holding them both tight.

"I had my gun," Hope blurted out.

Emily knew she still felt guilty for having the gun without Shawn around.

"I know," Shawn said to her softly. "And I'm very proud of you for handling things."

Relief washed over Hope's face as she hugged Shawn again.

"So, are you going to take a day to rest, or did you make her tell you everything?" Will asked, glancing at Emily.

"I've rested enough," Shawn said, standing up and turning to Alec. "I'm so sorry, brother."

"It's because of you that my kids were able to be safe," Alec said. "I can ask for no greater gift than that."

"I understand a training program is being set up for the adults," Shawn said, looking toward Will and Dillon.

"I think we've got it under control," Will nodded.

"He'll still butt in and take over," Dillon laughed.

"Not today," Shawn said, walking back to Emily and taking her hand. "Today, I will be at home with my family."

"So, tomorrow?" Dillon teased.

"Yeah," Shawn nodded as he led them home.

Chapter 15

Emily enjoyed their day of family time. Hope and Steven talked his ear off, informing him of everything he had missed. Shawn listened to every detail and enjoyed his time with them.

"Alright," Shawn said as Hope let a yawn escape. "It's way past your bedtime."

"Can we sleep with you?" Steven asked as he yawned.

"Not tonight," Shawn said, shaking his head. "I need you both well-rested to help with the adults' training."

"Really?" Steven smiled.

"Only if you guys get to bed," Shawn smiled back.

Immediately, both kids took off, running towards the stairs. It wasn't long before their voices summoned Shawn and Emily up to tuck them in.

"Where are you sleeping?" Shawn asked Marley once they were back out in the hall.

"He'll wander between them all night," Emily said. "Last night, he spent most of the night in the hall."

"Probably feels bad he didn't catch Chad and Veronica," Shawn said as he petted Marley's head. "But he needs to stop blaming himself, too."

Emily knew that he was referring to her

blaming herself for the sniper.

"Come on," Emily said, taking his hand. "Doc said you needed to rest."

Shawn didn't argue as she led him into the bedroom. Shawn stopped inside the room and pulled Emily into him, kissing her.

"You're supposed to rest," Emily smiled up at him.

"But I'm not tired," Shawn grinned back.

Emily knew that grin all too well at this point.

"I said rest," Emily laughed. "Not sleep."

"I'll rest better if I'm relaxed," Shawn grinned.

Before Emily could respond, Shawn lifted her off the ground. Emily laughed as she wrapped her legs around his waist.

"I missed you," Shawn said as he pulled her into another kiss.

Emily couldn't argue with him anymore. She missed him, too, and couldn't resist this moment.

Emily woke up and felt the empty bed beside her. She couldn't help but panic. Had she dreamed everything? She looked over and saw that the blankets were still messed up and Shawn's indent on the pillow. Emily jumped out of bed and quickly made her way downstairs.

"She only really slept after Doc yelled at her," Dillon said in the kitchen. "He told her it was either six hours of sleep, or she couldn't give you more blood."

"What did you do?" Shawn laughed.

"I sat in the hall and made sure she slept," Dillon replied. "I knew you would kill me if she didn't and got hurt."

"I wouldn't kill you," Shawn replied in a devilish tone. "But there are a few forms of torture I've always wanted to try."

"No one's torturing anyone," Emily said as she walked into the kitchen. "Why didn't you wake me up?"

"I thought you could use the rest, and apparently, I was right," Shawn smiled.

Emily shot a look at Dillon, who simply shrugged.

"He's bigger," Dillon replied as he took a bite of food. "His punches will hurt a lot more."

"But you'll see his attack coming," Emily smiled. "Remember, I cook most of the food around here."

Dillon stopped mid-bite and looked down at his plate.

Shawn let out a loud laugh that warmed Emily's heart. She had missed that sound.

"You two were made for each other," Dillon said after a moment.

Emily walked over and took a coffee cup that Shawn was offering her.

"Where are the kids?" Emily asked.

"They left for school a little bit ago," Shawn replied as she sat down. "I told them they could help me after."

Emily nodded with a smile as Shawn set her breakfast in front of her. She waited until he sat down with his plate before eating. Dillon went down to the basement, leaving them alone in the kitchen.

"Jessica dropped off our masks," Shawn said as he began to eat. "I made sure the kids took them just in case."

"Good," Emily nodded. "It's been a few days since the attack, so he could come back at any time."

"What does he say when you talk to him?" Shawn asked as he continued to eat.

"I don't," Emily replied. "I was done giving him the satisfaction. Sarah said, he mostly demands to speak with me, and when he gets no reply starts asking us to surrender people."

"You quit talking to him?" Shawn said with one eyebrow raised.

"I had better things to do," Emily shrugged. "Plus, you told me not to." "But you still did," Shawn pointed out.

"Better late than never," Emily grinned.

Shawn laughed as he finished his breakfast. Emily quickly cleaned up their dishes. She had just finished when Dillon came back upstairs.

"Ready to tell us all the things we did wrong?" Dillon grinned at Shawn.

"Always," Shawn said, standing up.

Emily smiled as she followed the two of them outside with Marley.

"We set up two shifts," Dillon was explaining. "That way, things could still run while training is happening."

"Good," Shawn nodded as they walked towards the group standing on the main street.

"We thought we would focus mainly on self-defense like you did with the kids," Dillon continued.

"We don't want them running and hiding like the kids," Shawn replied. "We need them ready to defend."

"Of course," Dillon nodded. "But if they can't defend themselves, then they can't defend anyone else."

Emily could see the pride on Shawn's face as he looked at Dillon. He wouldn't outright say it, but Dillon and Will had devised a good plan.

"Alright," Shawn nodded. "I'll watch and see what you guys come up with."

Dillon smiled as he ran off to stand next to Will.

"He has a good plan," Emily said as Shawn wrapped his arm around her.

"Yeah," Shawn nodded. "But can he pull it off?"

Emily shook her head and turned her attention back to the group. Will and Dillon were breaking everyone up into groups when a sound she remembered well echoed through Sanctuary.

"What the fuck?!" Shawn said with panic in his voice.

"They're ramming the gate with a tank again," Emily said, frustrated.

"Again?!" Shawn said as another crashing sound rang out.

Emily nodded her head and walked with him to the COM building. She led Shawn over to the monitor and pointed at the screen. There was the tank backing up to hit the gate once more.

"The kids will be on their way to the cellar, and he will keep going until someone talks to him," Emily explained.

"Really?" Shawn said with a big grin.

Emily eyed him, trying to figure out what he was thinking.

"May I?" Shawn asked, stepping forward.

"Go ahead," Emily said, taking a step back.

"Bring that bitch now!" The General's voice rang back.

"She's busy right now," Shawn replied. "But maybe I can help."

"Shawn?" The General couldn't hide the surprise in his voice. "How are you…."

"Alive?" Shawn finished for him. "You know, a little surgery and a long nap."

"That's not possible," The General gasped.

"I assure you it is," Shawn laughed. "Now, can you tell me what you want so I can say no already?"

"I'm sure you are aware of the present I delivered last time I was here?" The General said, steadying himself.

"I am," Shawn replied. "Have you come to give us another gift?"

"I'm here for what I asked for," The General spat. "Gather the others and come out here. No one else needs to be hurt."

"You can have your daughter and Chad," Shawn replied. "No one else."

The General was quiet for a moment. This was more than they had ever offered him before.

"You threatening to throw her off the wall again?" The General asked.

"Nope," Shawn replied. "You can take them both and go."

"Fine," The General nodded. "Send them out."

"Their already out there," Shawn answered.

Emily could see the evil smile on his face as he looked at The General's confusion.

"Where?" The General demanded.

"You should see where something was burned," Shawn explained. "That's her and Chad.

Emily watched as The General's gaze turned towards the burned area. Sadness crossed his features before rage overtook them.

"That's not her!" The General spat.

Emily could see the anger boiling in his face. She knew he wouldn't be happy. But she couldn't help the worry that built inside her.

"Maybe you could answer something for us," Shawn said to The General. "Who helped them get out and drop their phone?"

The General was still staring at where his daughter's body had been burned. Emily knew he wouldn't answer.

"You'll pay for this," The General sneered, turning back towards the monitor.

"No," Shawn said firmly. "She paid for the twenty-seven lives we lost in your crazy quest for power."

"Is my grandson in that pile?" The General asked coldly.

"My son is safe," Shawn replied. "Now, get your men, the fuck out of here before they join her."

Emily suddenly had an idea. She quickly leaned over to Cole.

"Pour some Kerosene over the wall," she said softly.

Cole's eyes widen in understanding. He grabbed Alec and Sam and made his way quickly outside.

"What are you going to do from in there?" The General asked, his face red with anger.

Emily placed her hand on Shawn's shoulder. He looked back at her and seemed to understand she wanted him to wait. A few minutes later, Emily and Shawn watched as the Kerosene began to pour on The General and the soldiers closest to him.

"What the fuck?!" The General yelled, trying to shield himself. "Someone take them out!"

"We can't get a shot, sir," one of the soldiers replied.

The General seemed to suddenly realize what they were covered in. Emily couldn't help but smile as panic spread across his face.

"Need a light?" Shawn asked him with a grin.

"Fall back!" The General yelled with panic in his voice. "Fall back!"

The soldiers and bikers began to quickly make their way back up the logging road.

"You know we couldn't light them with the tank so close," Shawn said, turning and pulling Emily close to him.

"Yeah," Emily nodded. "But he didn't know if we would risk the tank exploding or not."

"He'll be back," Shawn said softly.

"And we will be ready," Emily said with confidence.

"About time," Dillon smiled as he walked back into the COM building.

"What are you talking about?" Emily asked.

"You," Dillon smiled. "It's about time you had your fight back."

"I've been ready to fight," Emily said, offended.

"Out of duty," Dillon said. "Now you have your actual fight back."

Emily stood in silence for a moment and thought about what he said. It was true that she hadn't been herself lately. Dillon was right. There was something different about how she felt this time.

"She just needed him," Will said, walking in with a smile. "Now, can we get back to work?"

Dillon nodded and followed Will back out into the street.

"We'll be ready," Shawn said to her as he pulled her close. "We'll be together."

"Forever," Emily said as she hugged him back.

"Now, let's go make sure everyone else is ready," Shawn said as he let her go.

Emily walked with Shawn and Marley back outside and watched the training. A few minutes later, she heard the children returning to school. She couldn't wait for the day they no longer had to go into hiding. She turned her attention back to the training session. Julia was paired with Sam, and Sarah was training with Joe. Each of them got a few good shots in on their partner.

Emily felt herself focusing on Sarah and Joe. She wasn't sure when it happened or how she had missed it. They talked to each other with subtle laughs and puppy dog eyes. It was obvious to anyone with eyes that they were in a relationship.

"When did that happen?" Emily asked herself.

"He's been trying since he got here," Shawn laughed. "But I think he finally wore her down when we were outside the wall."

"Does everyone know?" Emily asked, turning to him.

"Pretty much," Shawn laughed. "They haven't said anything, but it's pretty obvious she has him wrapped around her finger."

Emily felt a smile spread across her face. She couldn't help but be happy for her brother.

"That's what you do here," Shawn said, wrapping his arm around her. "You built a place where people can find each other."

"That's what we have to protect," Emily replied.

Julia threw a punch right at that moment that caught Sam square in the nose. Emily couldn't help but laugh as Sam immediately covered his nose as his eyes began to water.

"I'm sorry," Julia said, rushing toward her husband.

"Don't be," Sam said after blinking a few times. "You hit one of those commandoes like that, and the war will be over."

Julia's face turned red as she smiled slightly.

Emily watched as the first group finished and the second group filed in. Shawn seemed pleased with the training.

"Your turn," Shawn said as he stood up and offered her his hand.

"Me?" Emily said as she took it.

"Couldn't hurt to practice," Shawn smiled at her.

Emily followed him out into the street and joined the others.

"Plus, it will be good for morale for them to see us training, too," Shawn smiled. "Just take it easy on me."

"No promises," Emily grinned.

For the next few hours, she worked through the training with Shawn. She knew he was holding back when they sparred, but didn't say anything. For now, she knew she needed the confidence boost and was willing to accept it.

"Alright," Will said as he ended the training. "We will all meet again tomorrow."

"You guys did good," Shawn said, walking over to Will and Dillon. "But I think we should get everyone together at once tomorrow."

"Do a drill," Will said, nodding in agreement.

"We know you guys can handle it," Shawn nodded in agreement. "Maybe have them be the enemy and see how everyone handles it."

"You want the kids in it?" Dillon asked.

"Yeah," Shawn nodded. "Everyone, just to make sure it doesn't turn to chaos."

"What about Margaret?" Emily said as everyone walked away.

She couldn't help but notice Margaret watching each of the training sessions. However, with her ability to walk severely limited, she couldn't join. But Emily knew Margaret would never go and hide in the cellar with the children.

"They got snipers," Shawn replied. "We should have our own setup."

"But it's not safe on the wall," Emily replied.

"We could set her up in one of the apartments," Shawn suggested. She would have a clear view and protect our people from above."

"How would she get up there?" Emily asked. "She couldn't run."

"We'll figure it out," Shawn assured her. "Sarah had an idea about putting one of those electric chairs on the wall to help Margaret up and down. Maybe she could install it on the apartment's stairs instead."

"I'll talk to her about it tomorrow," Emily said, glancing over at Sarah.

Sarah and Joe seemed to be having a moment over in front of the COM building. Emily couldn't bring herself to interrupt it. Moments of happiness were becoming rare, and she didn't want to spoil this one.

"Let's go get the kids," Shawn said as he took her hand. "We've got time to figure this out tomorrow."

"Good idea," Emily said as he led her toward the school.

They arrived just as the children began to pour out of the doors.

"He came back, didn't he?" Steven said, running towards them with Hope.

"He did," Emily nodded. "But he's gone now."

"Why can't he just leave us alone?" Hope huffed.

"It won't always be like this," Emily assured them.

Hope and Steven both looked defeated. Emily felt hurt that her words had not provided them with more comfort.

"It will be over soon," Shawn said beside her. "You two need to focus on school and training."

"I thought we were going to get to help with that," Hope said, putting her hands on her hips.

"Tomorrow," Shawn laughed. "The adults needed some time to be ready for your level of skills."

Steven and Hope both grinned. Emily walked home with her family, Marley happily leading the way. Once inside, everything seemed normal again. The kids were happy, Shawn was home, and the war outside seemed not to exist.

Chapter 16

The next day, the kids woke up early and were eager for their training session with the adults.

"It's not until this afternoon," Shawn groaned as he rolled over in bed.

"Come on," Emily laughed as she got out of bed. "We might as well get up."

Shawn groaned again but pulled himself out of bed. They quickly made their way through the morning routine and headed out into town. Despite it being a Saturday, everyone was up early and getting work done. Emily knew they all wanted to rest as soon as training was over.

"Why don't you guys go make sure everything else is in order?" Emily said to Shawn, Dillon, and the kids. "I'm going to go talk to Sarah about our sniper."

"We'll see you in a bit," Shawn said as he kissed her.

Emily made her way to the COM building and found both Sarah and Margaret were already there.

"Good morning," Emily smiled as she walked in. "You gals ready for today?"
"Sure am," Sarah nodded.

Emily could see the disappointment on Margaret's face as she said nothing.

"We were thinking and realized we were

wasting a valuable resource," Emily said. "Margaret, we would like to set up one of the apartments as your sniper's nest."

"I appreciate it, dear," Margaret said with a forced smile. "But there is no way I could make it up there to be of any use."

"Maybe you could," Emily said as she looked at Sarah.

"The chair!" Sarah said with excitement. "I had it ready for the wall, but it could quickly be put into the stairwell."

"There's no need to go through the trouble," Margaret insisted. "There is so much other work to do."

"And having you up there might save our lives," Emily insisted. "Unless you think you couldn't do the job."

The look on Margaret's face told Emily she had struck a nerve.

"I can do it," Margaret insisted.

"Then it's settled," Emily smiled.

"I'll get that put in right away," Sarah grinned. "It should be ready before training. What time is training?"

"Don't know," Emily shrugged.

"How do you not know?" Sarah looked at her with suspicion.

"You'll see," Emily said, walking towards Margaret. "May I?"

Margaret moved back from the radio and turned it to the inside speakers.

"Attention," Emily said into the microphone. "As of today, we will have random drills with all members of Sanctuary involved. The time will not be announced. Anyone wearing a vest is a member of the enemy team. Our job is to stop them and survive. Please go about your day as usual until given notice that it has begun."

"That's going to keep everyone on edge," Sarah said as Emily finished.

"They're already on edge," Emily replied. "But this way, they will be ready."

"Well, I'd better get to work on the chair," Sarah grinned as she headed towards the door.

"Tell Joe I said hi," Emily smiled back at her.

"How…" Sarah said, stopping and turning. "We were going to tell you after all this was over."

"Don't worry about it," Emily laughed. "You both seem happy, and that's all I care about."

"I just thought with him being your brother and all…." Sarah stopped and looked ashamed.

"With him being my brother, I'll warn him that if he hurts you, I can get rid of a body," Emily smiled.

Sarah laughed and quickly headed out of the COM building.

"Kids," Margaret said, shaking her head.

Emily walked back out of the COM building with Marley. Everyone did seem a bit on edge, but nothing concerning.

"All ready?" Emily asked as she walked toward Shawn and the kids.

"Almost," Shawn smiled at her.

"We'd better get going," Hope smiled.

"Where are you going?" Emily asked her.

"The bakery," Steven replied. "We can't leave Bobby alone again."

"Plus, that's where we would normally be today," Hope added.

"Then you'd better get going," Emily smiled at them.

Emily watched as the kids took off, running towards the bakery.

"Are you ready for this?" Shawn asked beside her.

Emily didn't reply as she thought. Her mind returned to when Dillon asked if she was The General in Sanctuary. She had cringed at the comparison, but it was accurate. Only, instead of leading her people into a pointless battle and being willing to sacrifice their lives, it was her job to keep them all safe.

"Just remember," Shawn said softly. "It isn't your job to save everyone."

"But to make sure they can save themselves," Emily replied. "When are we doing this?"

"I don't know," Shawn shrugged. "Will has pulled the guys between the walls and will do it at random. It's best if none of us are prepared."

"So, what am I supposed to do?" Emily pouted at him.

"Whatever you would normally do," Shawn shrugged.

"I need you to get the sniper rifles and ammo up to the apartment. I'll get the key and give it to Margaret," Emily nodded.

"You think it will be ready in time?" Shawn asked, raising his eyebrow.

"We need to be prepared if it is," Emily sighed.

"Alright," Shawn nodded. "I need you to come with me first, though."

Emily looked at him, confused as he pulled her towards the armory.

"We found a stash of these a while back," Shawn said, opening a crate. "I thought it would be a good idea for our trial run."

Emily watched as Shawn reached in and pulled out a paintball gun.

"I'll make sure everyone armed right now has one," Shawn continued. "All of Will's guys already do."

"You sure about this?" Emily said, turning the gun over in her hands.

"We want it to be as real as possible," Shawn nodded. "Also, Dillon is with Will. With him knowing how The General worked, it just made the most sense."

"Okay," Emily nodded.

"You go get that key, and I'll take care of things here," Shawn said, pulling more guns out of the crate.

Emily turned and headed back home with Marley. She found the apartment key and headed back to Margaret. She stopped by the apartments on the way and was surprised to see that Sarah and Joe had almost finished the chair.

"She's a slave driver," Joe said as soon as he saw Emily.

"You'd better be good to her," Emily warned him with a smile. "I've come to like her more than you."

"That hurts," Joe said, covering his heart with his hand.

"No more than you not telling me," Emily quickly replied, winking at Sarah. "I…we thought…." Joe stuttered.

"You better have told Mom," Emily replied. "Otherwise, Sarah here will end up single again."

"She knows," Sarah laughed.

"She does?!" Joe said, surprised.

"She knew the day we redid the house," Sarah said, shaking her head. "I think Emily was the last one to figure it out."

"I've had a lot going on," Emily said, rolling her eyes.

"We know," Sarah grinned. "But it's nice not trying to hide it anymore."

"I was going to tell you," Joe said, looking embarrassed.

"You can make it up to me by finishing this chair," Emily smiled at him.

Joe nodded and quickly got back to work. Emily left the two of them to it and headed back to the COM building.

"Here's the key," Emily said as she walked in. "Shawn is setting up what you need, but there will also be a paintball gun for the practice run."

"That will be fun," Margaret laughed, taking the key.

"Shawn wants to make it as real as possible," Emily smiled.

"I'll sound the alarm through the speakers before I leave here," Margaret said. "But I did think of something."

"What's that?" Emily said, sitting down beside her.

"The only way they could get in is through the emergency exits or the front gate," Margaret began. "We tend to leave the inner gate open all the time. It would be their biggest entry point."

"Good point," Emily nodded. "I'll make sure to take care of that."

Margaret smiled with pride as she tucked the key into her pocket. Emily spent the next several hours checking in with everyone. They were all aware of the paintball guns and how their role would change if shot. They would become zombies, changing sides and trying to take out the other townspeople. The kids were excited by the new rules. It was like all of Sanctuary would be playing one giant game.

Emily was walking the main street when the alarm sounded through the speakers. She looked at the gate and saw the bikers slowly making their way in.

"Show time," Emily said to Marley as she ran off.

Emily reached the gate in a matter of minutes and quickly closed it; half the bikers were stuck on the wrong side. She turned back just in time to see Margaret duck into the apartment stairwell. Joe and Sarah had finished the chair. Emily smiled, knowing that she was on her way to her position.

"You going to make it that easy?" Will said, making her jump.

She turned to see his paintball gun aimed directly at her. Marley let out a growl that made him hesitate and take a step back. Emily acted quickly and shot him with her paintball gun. Will looked down at the paint splatter in shock.

"Nope," Emily smiled as she walked over and touched his head. "Now, you lie down."

Will grinned as he took his position as a dead body on the ground. Emily quickly made her way up the street, helping a few people caught off guard and turning a few out there into zombies. It seemed like this went on for hours, but in reality, it had only been minutes. Margaret was even good with her paintball gun from a distance, catching more of the bikers by surprise.

Suddenly, the alarm turned off, and Shawn was calling everyone's attention. He had not participated in the drill, but took it upon himself to ensure the rules were followed and knew when to end it.

"Wow," Shawn said, smiling as they gathered around him. "The enemy was stopped in less than fifteen minutes."

Everyone smiled with pride as he spoke.

"Though it wasn't without losses," Shawn continued. "Ten people were turned and put down."

Emily frowned at the number. Even though she knew it was impossible, she didn't want to lose anyone.

"I think we all know we are not going to get through this without casualties, but we want the number to be as low as possible," Shawn continued. "With this being the first time we've been in this situation, I'm impressed."

She looked around and saw that everyone seemed happy with themselves.

"We should continue this over the next few days," Shawn said. "No warning, just like today."

"I'll live next time," Cole spoke up. "I'm tired of always getting bitten."

Everyone let out a slight laugh at his frustration.

"I have to say, Emily did something we didn't expect," Will said, stepping forward. "Her shutting that gate as quickly as she did locked half our guys out."

Emily couldn't help but blush at the compliment.

"Then she took out their leader and kept going," Will continued.

"She took you out," Shawn let out a slight laugh.

"I had her," Will defended himself. "But Marley decided to be part of the game, and she took advantage."

Emily reached down and petted Marley's head. He had been careful to only use his bark and growl, seeming to know that this wasn't a real fight.

"You're telling me it wouldn't work on the soldiers?" Emily asked with a grin.

"You got me there," Will nodded.

"Who shot me?" one of the bikers, Greg, asked.

Emily smiled, looking at him. His paint splatter was directly over his heart.

"Sniper," Emily grinned, glancing at Margaret.

Emily could see that Margaret was beaming with pride.

"We'll think of a better plan next time," Will smiled.

"And we'll be ready," Margaret grinned.

"That we will," Shawn agreed.

"Also, don't forget to pick up your chickens!" Jessica yelled out.

Emily realized she had not picked up theirs yet. Thanksgiving was only a few days away, and she had nearly forgotten about it. Her eyes immediately went to Alec. He stood with his children, and she saw the pain on his face.

"Alec," Emily called as she jogged over to him.

"We did well today," Alec said with a fake smile.

"We did," Emily nodded in agreement. "But I actually wanted to talk to you about something else.

"You guys head home," Alec said to the children. "I'll be right behind you."

Emily smiled at the kids as they began to walk toward their house.

"What do you need?" Alec asked.

"I wanted to invite you guys to join us for Thanksgiving dinner," Emily smiled at him.

Alec looked surprised at her invitation.

"I don't know," he said nervously.

"I know you can't boil water, let alone cook a chicken," Emily laughed.

"You're right," Alec let out a small smile as a tear slid down his face. "But it's supposed to be a time for family and…."

"We are family," Emily assured him. "Please, come to dinner at my place."

Alec studied her face for a minute, the pain glaring through his eyes.

"What time?" Alec asked with a forced smile.

"Come over about noon," Emily grinned. "Dinner should be ready about five, but we always gather early."

"We'll be there," Alec nodded.

Emily turned to head back to where Shawn was waiting for her.

"Emily!" Alec called after her, causing her to stop and turn back. "Thank you," Alec said with a genuine smile.

"We'll see you at noon," Emily smiled back.

With that, Alec turned to follow his kids home, and Emily headed back to Shawn.

"What was that about?" Shawn asked as she walked toward him.

"I invited them to dinner," Emily explained.

"Always thinking of everyone else," Shawn said softly as he pulled her close. "I'm honestly surprised you don't try to fit everyone into our dining room."

"You think there's a room?" Emily smiled up at him.

"No," Shawn laughed. "It would be a Thanksgiving massacre."

Emily laughed with him as they headed back up the street.

"So, was today better or worse than you thought it would be?" Emily asked.

"Better," Shawn nodded. "You closing that gate took out half of the fight before it started."

"Margaret pointed it out," Emily admitted. "I was going to close it sooner, but didn't want to give them a chance to develop a new plan."

"Smart," Shawn nodded. "You caught them off guard."

"Any major issues I should know about?" Emily asked as they reached the house.

"Nothing too bad," Shawn replied as they walked onto the porch. "Hope and I need to have a conversation, though."

"What did she do?" Emily asked as she stopped just outside the door.

"The kids were all safe, just like they should have been," Shawn sighed, rubbing his neck. "Howard got pinned down, and she rushed outside to help him. Three other people were "killed" trying to protect her."

"She's not supposed to run out," Emily said in shock. "She knows that!"

"Yeah," Shawn nodded. "I wonder where she gets it from?"

Emily frowned at him as he spoke. She knew that he was referring to her.

"She's going to have a nice little bruise to remind her of her mistake," Shawn continued.

"Was she…?" Emily began.

"I told the guys not to hold back," Shawn nodded. "She took a paintball right to the chest."

"So, what she did led to four of our ten deaths?" Emily asked.

"Yup," Shawn nodded. "When, at most, it would have been one."

Emily could understand why Hope ran out to help. She wanted, just like Emily, to save everyone she could.

"Luckily, Steven and Bobby got back inside just in time, or they would have been taken out," Shawn continued.

"They couldn't leave her alone because of the buddy system," Emily said.

"Yeah," Shawn nodded. "She not only risked her life but theirs."

"We should talk to her together," Emily said after a moment. "Along with Steven and Bobby."

"You think?" Shawn asked.

"Of course," Emily replied. "She put their lives at risk, too. They should be able to tell her how they feel about it."

"That may help get through her stubbornness," Shawn looked at her with a smile. "Another lovely trait she got from…."

"I know," Emily interrupted him, rolling her eyes. "You go in, and I'll go get Bobby."

"Yes, ma'am," Shawn smiled as he opened the door.

Emily found Bobby and discovered he was very angry about what Hope had done. Julia and Sam had no problem with Bobby coming and discussing the situation with Hope. Shawn gathered them all in the living room. Emily could tell by the look on Hope's face that she was ready to defend what she did.

"Alright," Shawn began. "I think we need to talk about what happened today."

"I'm not sorry," Hope blurted out. "I would do it again to save Howard."

"And what about the three other people who died trying to save you?" Shawn asked softly.

"They didn't have to do that," Hope said, crossing her arms and leaning back.

"And neither did you," Emily pointed out.

"And what about Steven and Bobby?" Shawn asked. "Their job is to stay with you no matter what, and you led them straight into danger."

"They were fine," Hope huffed. "I'm the one who got shot."

"Which means we failed!" Bobby yelled. "It's our job to keep each other safe, and you got shot!"

Hope looked up at him, surprised by his tone.

"We know it was pretend," Steven spoke up. "But I still cried when we went inside."

"Which means I went from two people watching my back to none," Bobby said firmly.

"You left us alone!"

Hope straightened up and looked between the two of them.

"I'm sorry," Hope said, barely above a whisper.

"This time, you get the chance to be sorry," Steven pointed out.

"But next time could be real," Bobby added.

Emily could see that Hope's defensive wall had shattered around her. Hearing what Bobby and Steven had to say was getting through to her way more than Emily or Shawn could have.

"We risk as few lives as possible," Emily said to Hope. "You are supposed to help protect three of them, yourself included."

"I know," Hope said, looking ashamed. "I just wanted to win, and I didn't think. I'm really sorry."

"You promise not to do it again?" Bobby asked her.

"I promise," Hope nodded. "Can you forgive me?"

"Always," Steven grinned. "But next time...."

"Next time, we'll let you have it," Bobby smiled.

The two boys pulled Hope into a hug. Emily saw that Hope winced slightly at the tight embrace. She knew it was pain from the fresh bruise from where the paintball hit her. Once the kids finished, Bobby headed home, and the kids went upstairs.

"Um, I think you blamed the wrong parent for what she did today," Emily said to Shawn once they were alone.

"Excuse me?" Shawn said with surprise.

"She didn't want to lose," Emily pointed out. "That's the competitiveness she learned from you."

"I am not competitive," Shawn insisted as Dillon walked in.

"Yes, you are," Dillon said as he walked to the kitchen.

"Hey!" Shawn said as he turned towards Dillon's direction.

Emily said nothing as she waited for him to turn back to her.

"Alright," Shawn sighed. "Maybe I'm a little competitive."

Chapter 17

They continued to have drills over the next few days. Emily had tried to talk Shawn out of having one on Thanksgiving, but he refused. He insisted that the General could return anytime, and they needed to be ready. She was surprised when they made it through dinner without the alarm sounding. Alec and his children arrived, and though Emily could still feel their sadness, she hoped they had brought some joy to their holiday.

"I should get them to bed," Alec said, standing up. "They look like they're about to pass out, and I don't want to carry both of them home."

Alec and his kids were the only ones left as Emily's family, and Will had already left for the night.

"Thanks for having us," Alec smiled at Emily.

"We expect to see you next year," Emily grinned as she hugged him.

"You keep cooking like that, and we might just have to move in," Alec teased.

Emily and Shawn walked them to the door and waved goodbye. Emily had just sat down on the couch when the alarm went off.

"Really?" Emily said to Shawn.

Suddenly, the alarm made two loud beeps and then continued.

"It wasn't me," Shawn said, walking towards the door.

They didn't want anyone confused if the real alarm went off, so they changed it in case of an emergency. The two loud beeps would interrupt the alarms every thirty seconds. Before Emily could reply, the sounds of explosions overhead began.

"Mommy!" Hope yelled as she and Steven ran down the stairs with their gas masks on.

Bobby suddenly burst through their door, wearing his mask.

"Get to someplace safe," Emily said to them as she grabbed her weapons.

"And stay there," Shawn warned them as he walked out their door, his mask in his hand.

Emily followed, not taking the time to put hers on either.

"Flares," Dillon said, walking up beside them.

"Why would he shoot up flares?" Emily asked, looking around.

Everyone was already preparing for the worst on the main street. Instead of the paintball guns, each was armed and ready to defend their home.

"We'll worry about that later," Shawn said sternly. "I don't think he's here to give us a fireworks show."

Emily knew he was right. While the rockets last time had deadly consequences, they were also meant to be a distraction. She turned her attention away from the street and to the wall. Every several feet, black lines were drawn from the top of the wall. Emily focused on one of the lines as it shifted in the breeze.

"Are those ropes?" Emily asked.

Shawn and Dillon's gaze immediately followed hers.

"They're not coming through," Shawn said through gritted teeth. "They're coming over."

Everything suddenly made sense. The snipers took their guards off the wall. This meant that no one would see them climbing up. That is also how the phone got dropped. One of the soldiers must have dropped it in his hurry to get back over the wall before being seen. The General had been toying with them, and he was done playing.

Emily looked to her left to see a group of people moving silently through the street. She recognized them as soldiers immediately. She reached up and grabbed Shawn's arm to get his attention. Shawn looked down at her and then looked at where she was staring. Shawn got Dillon's attention immediately. They seemed to change as they silently made their way off the porch and towards the soldiers, signaling for Emily to wait.

Emily held her breath as she watched them sneak up on the soldiers. The people in the street ahead were wearing their masks, and most of their attention had been drawn to the sky. Another bright burst of light revealed Shawn and Dillon to the soldiers. As soon as the light was on them, the guys moved quickly. They took down the group of six in a moment, but not before one of the soldiers could fire a shot.

Everyone's attention was drawn back to the ground as groups of soldiers and bikers emerged. Emily felt her hands shake slightly as she held her gun.

"Help the kids," Emily said quickly to Marley.

Marley didn't seem happy about the command but moved back to stand by the door. With the streets already swarming with the enemy, Emily wanted to make sure they made it to safety. She took off down the stairs and followed Shawn and Dillon. The street would have been dark if not for the continued explosions overhead.

Emily didn't have time to look at faces as she fought her way up the street. The light from the flares shone against the blood pooling in the street. Emily ensured that each soldier or biker she killed wouldn't get back up. However, some were still being missed. As she continued to fight, the growl of zombies began to mix into the chaos.

Emily had lost sight of Shawn and Dillon as they worked their way into the fight. Without Marley, she felt alone for the first time while having to fight. Emily kept going, though, refusing to give up or be scared.

"Bitch!" One of the soldiers yelled as he slashed at her with a knife.

Emily made no sound as the knife quickly cut through the soft flesh of her arm. She instead raised her gun and fired without a second thought. The soldier dropped to the ground, blood flowing from the bullet hole in his forehead. Emily heard a sound that grabbed her attention. She lifted her gun to fire again.

Emily could see Marley growling and snapping at people outside the town hall. All the blood left her face as she saw all the kids in Sanctuary behind him. The doors to the town hall are shattered, and several dead soldiers are on the steps. Emily knew it was one of the kids' backup hiding spots if they couldn't make it to the cellar or the garage.

Emily spotted Shawn and Will not far from her, fighting a combination of soldiers and bikers. No one else seems to have noticed what is happening. Emily felt her blood boil as she watched The General approach the kids.

"Shawn!" Emily yelled as she tried to make her way toward the children.

Shawn glanced at her and then looked towards the town hall.

"Will, the kids!" Shawn yelled as he saw what was happening.

Shawn and Will both began to fight their way toward the kids. However, their path continued to be blocked. Emily felt her panic rising as her movement slowed, getting to the kids. One of the soldiers had grabbed Hope by the arm while Marley was busy biting at another.

"Hope!" Emily heard herself scream in fear.

Suddenly, Dillon appeared, breaking the soldier's arm and freeing Hope.

"Get to Margaret!" Dillon yelled at the kids as he continued to fight.

The kids took off at a run, disappearing into the stairwell moments later. Emily continued to fight with everything she had to reach Dillon and Marley. She was nearly there when The General reached where Dillon was.

"There you are," The General said casually. "Now, where did you send my grandson?"

"Fuck you," Dillon yelled as he swung at The General.

Emily gasped as The General didn't hesitate and shot Dillon in the stomach. Dillon fell back immediately, landing on the stairs and holding his stomach.

"Such a waste," The General said with no emotion.

Emily finally broke through the fight and ran to Dillon.

"The kids," Dillon coughed, looking up at her.

"They're safe," Emily assured him.

"Unlike you," The General smiled at her.

"Don't," Dillon gasped, trying to grab onto her arm as she stood up.

"I have to admit, they are putting up more of a fight than I expected," The General said, looking at her. "If any survive, there are a few who might take."

Emily said nothing as she stared at him. She dropped her pistol to the ground. It had run out of ammo on her way over. The only defense she had left was the knife still on her hip. However, she didn't reach for it as she stared at The General.

"Time to end this," The General said as he motioned for her to come to him.

Emily stood firm and didn't move toward him.

"You had your fun," The General growled. "Now it's time to end this."

"You're right," Emily growled, noticing soldiers moving closer. "It is."

The soldiers quickly moved towards her. Emily pulled the knife from her waist and sliced him across the throat. Marley jumped and tore the throat out of the other.

"Clever," The General smiled. "But can you do it alone?"

Marley lunged at The General as he pulled his gun and fired another shot. Emily screamed as Marley fell to the ground, not moving.

"I never liked dogs," The General smiled, turning his attention back to her.

Emily glanced around at the fight that was still unfolding. She could see everyone trying to fight to get to her, but their paths were continually blocked. Finally, her eyes locked with Shawn, and she could see his panic. He and Will were trying with everything they had to reach her. Emily knew they wouldn't make it, not in time.

"I love you," Emily mouthed to Shawn.

She saw that his panic increased, and he fought harder. Emily forced herself to look away from him and back at The General. His eyes were cold and hard. A sick smile spread across his face as he moved closer to her. Emily held the knife firmly in her hand as he moved. "Haven't you tried that already?" The General said, motioning to the knife.

Emily knew he was referring to the last time she stabbed him. She knew she hadn't killed him then and that he would somehow survive. She wouldn't make that mistake again. One of them would die today, and she was determined it wouldn't be her.

Emily remained still and ready as The General came closer.

"Why don't you give that here before you hurt yourself?" The General sneered as he reached towards her.

Emily didn't hesitate as she moved the knife quickly, slicing The General's arm. The

General cried out in pain as he pulled back. The blood was already spilling down his arm from the deep cut.

"You'll pay for that," The General spat at her.

"Stop talking!" Emily yelled back.

She was tired of him monologuing like some evil villain on a Saturday morning cartoon.

The General moved fast, closing the distance been them. It caught Emily off guard, and she stumbled a few steps back. She had always seen him wait for others to handle his fights and thought he couldn't do it himself. She was proven wrong as his fist met the side of her face hard, knocking her down to one knee.

"I've had enough of this," The General said as he grabbed her ponytail and lifted her to her feet.

Emily quickly recovered from her shock and began to fight back. She ignored the pain in her scalp as she pulled back from his grip. The General stopped and looked back at her in frustration. Emily quickly seized the opportunity to slash at him again with the knife. The General quickly pulled back, releasing Emily's hair and causing her to miss.

"It won't be that easy," Emily glared at him as she prepared herself for the fight.

The General lunged at her, knocking her to the ground and causing her to drop the knife. Emily shielded her face as The General struck at her several times. She could tell that he was getting winded quickly. It had probably been years since he actually fought. Emily continued to shield herself and waited for her moment. Her arms were sore from the hits as The General finally lost momentum. She quickly seized the moment and hit him as hard as she could. The General was stunned for a moment, and Emily moved quickly. She pushed him off of her, kicking him in the head as she did so.

Emily turned and grabbed the knife she had dropped before climbing on top of The General. Emily pressed the knife to his throat and allowed the tip of it to puncture his skin, causing a small trickle of blood to form.

"You win," The General winced.

"You lose," Emily responded as she increased the pressure on the knife.

"Let me turn," The General said, catching her off guard. "Let me become one of them to serve you."

"The dead serve no one," Emily replied harshly.

The General looked like he wanted to speak, but Emily didn't give him a chance. She put full pressure on the knife as she glided it across his throat. The General made a few gurgling sounds before the light in his eyes was gone. Emily quickly lifted the knife and sank it into his eye. She looked up, soaked in blood, and could see the fear in the eyes of the soldiers closest to her. Emily stood slowly, still gripping her knife in her hand. The soldiers immediately stopped fighting, and each dropped the weapons, holding their hands in the air.

"Get on the fucking ground," Emily growled at them.

None spoke as they lay down on their stomachs on the blood-soaked ground. Emily turned and began to look for Shawn. She spotted him quickly, just a short distance away. Shawn grabbed Clint from behind, holding his arms. Clint struggled against his grip, and Will plunged a knife into his heart. Shawn released Clint and allowed his body to fall to the ground. Will quickly moved to stab him in the head.

Shawn's attention had already turned back to her, and he began to run toward her. Emily ran and jumped into his arms. The fighting around them had stopped as both groups' leaders were lying dead in the street.

"Are you okay?" Shawn asked, squeezing her tight.

"I'm fine," Emily assured him. "Is it over?"

"It's over," Shawn said as he kissed her.

The kiss was deep and filled with passion. Emily returned it in kind, forgetting the gruesome scene around them. When they pulled apart, Emily could see that everyone had already begun to clean up around them. Dillon and Marley were already in the clinic, and the remaining soldiers and bikers had been gathered in front of the town hall, each on their knees.

"What do you want to do about them?" Shawn asked, nodding towards the group.

"Are any of the bikers savable?" Emily asked him.

"No," Shawn said flatly.

"We still need someone to call in the remaining troops outside," Will said, walking towards them.

"No, we don't," Emily said as she walked towards the gate.

Everyone followed her except for the ones who remained to keep guard on the soldiers.

"Ready?" Emily asked as she reached the control panel.

Everyone seemed to understand her plan as they split into two groups on either side of the wall. Emily entered the code and opened the outer gate. Immediately, the remaining troops began to pour in, already celebrating their victory.

"Welcome to Sanctuary," Emily said as she closed the gate behind them once they all had entered. "I'm sorry you won't be staying long."

"Let's go," Will yelled as he led them to where the other troops were waiting.

Emily stopped them and saw a few people looking out of place with their wrists bound.

"Wait," Emily called out as she walked towards them with Shawn behind her. "Who are you?"

"We're not one of them," a man with a shaggy grey beard answered.

"But we're just as guilty," another answered.

"We didn't know," the grey-bearded man replied. "He tricked us, and after Robert escaped, he…."

"You're the scientists who worked with Robert," Emily said, looking between them all.

"Yes," the man answered, looking down. "We all played our part at the end of the world."

"Can you help fix it?" Emily asked them as she led them away from the soldiers and bikers.

"We can try," they all nodded in agreement.

"We have some cabins back through there," Emily pointed out. "Why don't you rest there, and I'll be there as soon as I'm done here."

They all looked at her in surprise as they turned and headed toward the quarantine area.

"It's a large group to lead out," Shawn said as she walked towards the group.

"Blood has already been spilled," Emily replied, not looking at him. "We end this now."

Shawn nodded in agreement as he followed her over to the group.

"Your leaders are dead," Emily said to them. "You came here with them willingly to destroy us. We had done nothing but try to find a way to live in a world that a madman created. There is no place in here or out there for you."

Emily nodded, and gunshots began to ring out. Within moments, the entire group was dead. Emily helped the others quickly ensure that none of them would rise again.

"Margaret," Emily said into her walkie. "Keep the kids up there." "Will do,"

Margaret responded.

"Let's get this trash cleaned up so we can tend to our own," Emily said to everyone.

Chapter 18

They all worked into the early morning hours to clean the dead out of the streets. Emily opened the gate, and they used the trucks to drive the bodies to the burn pits. Even with the bloodshed that night, only three of their own were killed. While their loss still came with a heavy weight, Emily knew they were lucky not to have lost more.

Doc had been held up in his clinic all night, tending to the wounded. There were many of those, but at least they survived. Dillon and Marley were, however, by far the worst of those who were injured. Doc had told them Dillon was lucky to survive, and he lost him several times during the surgery. Marley had taken the bullet to his right front leg near the shoulder. Doc had tried everything he could, but was left with only one choice. If they wanted Marley to live, he would have to lose the leg.

Emily agreed to amputate but had not had time to prepare herself for the struggle of helping Marley adjust. She knew there had been plenty of three-legged dogs before the apocalypse, and she was confident that Marley would adjust.

The first rays of the sun were just starting to light up Sanctuary, and Emily stood outside the clinic, looking at their once peaceful town. Though the bodies had been cleared away, the battle had left its mark. The street was still flowing with blood like a river. The town hall doors were still smashed, and blood splattered across the storefronts. Emily had worked so hard to keep bloodshed out of Sanctuary, and The General had made everything change.

All the kids stayed in the apartments while the adults worked to set the town right. Hope had explained that they were cut off while trying to get to the farm, and there was too much fighting to get to the garage. They weren't in the town hall long before the doors broke. They tried to fight back, but it was harder to do than when they practiced. Emily had assured them that she was proud of them, and they had done everything exactly how they were supposed to. It took them a while, but they all fell asleep around the apartment. Margaret and her husband had stayed with them while Emily returned to work.

"It's going to stain," Emily said as Shawn walked beside her. "This will be a scar that will never go away."

"It will heal," Shawn assured her as he wrapped his arms around her. "We survived."

"Not all of us," Emily said as she looked over at the coffins waiting outside the clinic.

"They died to protect this place," Shawn said. "Something that all of us were willing to die for."

"I'm tired of people dying," Emily sighed. "I just want us to live."

"Maybe we should go talk to the scientists," Shawn suggested.

"Robert made the formula," Emily said, looking towards the gate. "That's why The General wanted him. He's probably the only one who could reverse this."

"If I remember the journal correctly, there were only five scientists," Shawn said. "Robert and the woman died, leaving three."

"Yeah," Emily said.

She didn't understand where he was going with this.

"But we have four scientists back there," Shawn finished.

"Four?" Emily repeated.

She had been so caught up in the fight that she hadn't realized that there should have been three.

"Who's the fourth?" Emily asked.

"Let's go find out," Shawn said, taking her hand.

Emily walked with him back to the quarantine area. All scientists were sitting outside the first cabin as if waiting for her to arrive.

"Sorry it took me so long," Emily said as she walked toward them. "There was a lot of work to be done."

"No apologies needed," the man with the grey beard said as he stood up.

"If you all don't mind, I have a few questions for you," Emily said as she sat down.

"Of course," the man with the grey beard nodded as he sat.

"I assume all of you were part of the original research team with Robert," Emily said.

She watched as each of them nodded in agreement. She had to be sure they weren't just trying to claim something to save their lives.

"And what was the original purpose of that project?" she asked them.

"We were all trying in our way to save animals or plants that were in danger of or were already extinct," the man answered her with a soft smile. "Of course, that research was combined to make the dead walk the earth."

Shawn looked at Emily, and she could tell he believed what the man was saying.

"Forgive me," Emily smiled. "But I don't think I got any of your names."

"This is Gregory, Alex, and Michael," the man said, pointing to the others. "We lost Sylvia before the outbreak happened."

Robert had never named the others in his journal, none except for Sylvia. She found it odd that this man made sure to say her name.

"And you are?" Emily asked cautiously.

"Robert," the man smiled. "And may I say, you have made more out of this place than I ever dreamed possible. I thought it would be self-sufficient for a year, maybe two. But you have managed to make it so much more."

"That's not possible," Emily said in shock. "Robert is dead. He shot himself, and I buried him myself!"

"You buried me?" the man who called himself Robert smiled at her. "Why would you do that?"

"You can't be Robert!" Emily said, starting to feel angry.

Even though she had never met Robert, he still felt like a friend to her, and it angered her that this man would pretend to be him. Plus, why would he have kept demanding Emily send him out if The General had Robert?

"I assure you I am," the man who called himself Robert smiled. "I started this place as soon as I was clear of The General. It was nearly complete when the flash happened."

"And when Robert ended up alone, he took his own life!" Emily blurted out, with tears in her eyes.

"My assistant, Trevor, ended his life in the control room," Robert said softly. "I was the only one alive and saw military vehicles on the move. I feared the General would find me and use me again. I wrote the final entry, placed the journal with Trevor, and left."

"Why?" Emily asked him, still angry. "Why would you leave?"

"To keep things from getting worse," the man called Robert responded. "I did return, but the gates were closed. I looked up and could see you walking the wall. You looked so small and frail, but your baby belly was plainly visible."

"Why didn't you come to the gate?" Emily asked him.

She was starting to believe the man, but was still angry. How could he have just left her here alone?

"You looked to be alone and, in that state…." Robert began. "I feared you would kill me on sight or at least refuse to let me in to protect your child."

Emily knew that he wasn't wrong. She had vowed never to let anyone in once she closed the gates.

"I stayed close by, though," Robert continued. "I was here the day you opened the gate and let the first group in."

"You just watched?" Shawn spoke up.

Emily could tell he was just as confused as she was.

"Yes," Robert nodded. "I thought it best not to interfere."

"How did you end up with The General?" Emily spat at him.

"When the bikers showed up at the gate, I recognized a few of them. They were in charge of security at times in the original facility," Robert explained. "I wanted to help you try to protect what you built. I thought if I became part of their group, I could try to figure out how to destroy them from the inside."

"The General wasn't known for taking in people," Shawn said firmly.

"That he wasn't," Robert said, looking down. "They stumbled across me during one of the retreats. I convinced them I had escaped and was willing to help them."

"Is that how they learned about the emergency exits!?" Emily said through gritted teeth.

"I thought for sure you would have sealed them," Robert said with regret in his voice. "When I learned what happened, I was devastated."

"June died because of you!" Emily said, her anger boiling over.

"I am truly sorry," Robert said. "I had to tell them something to gain their trust, so I chose something I thought would prove useless."

"So, she died so you could save yourself!" Emily spat at him.

"I would much rather be dead," Robert said grimly. "But I can't leave this world like this."

"What do you mean?" Shawn asked as he rubbed Emily's arm, trying to calm her.

"I made it," Robert sighed. "I may be the only one who can unmake it."

"You think you can reverse this?" Emily gasped.

"I have to try," Robert said, looking back at her.

Emily stood up and walked out of the quarantine area. She had to get some air, to get away from him. Shawn followed right behind her and closed the door.

"I don't believe this," Emily said as soon as they were alone.

"I think he's telling the truth," Shawn said as he watched her pace.

"I do, too," Emily said with tears. "It doesn't help that June died because of him."

"What if he's right?" Shawn said, grabbing her arms. "What if he's the one who can stop what's going on?"

"So, I set up this place to work, and he gets to come back three years later and take over after hiding in the woods like a coward?"

"I don't want to take over," Robert said, walking through the door. "Sanctuary is yours. I'm merely asking to be part of it and try to fix my mistake."

Emily rolled her eyes as she turned away from him. She knew she was acting childish, but right now, she didn't care.

"I know I never met you," Emily said after a few moments. "But I always thought of you as a friend through your journals and everything."

"You are an amazing person," Robert said, stepping forward. "I've watched this place grow even from the outside. I realized you had read everything I left and were trying to honor me when I saw the sign."

"You have a grave," Emily said, turning towards him with tears in her eyes.

"We can change that to honor Trevor," Robert smiled. "It was his sacrifice that allowed all of this to happen."

Emily nodded as she wiped the tears from her face.

"I could have never made this place what you have," Robert continued. "I am smart, but when it comes to people, I am one of the stupidest people you will meet."

Emily looked at him as she continued to wipe her face.

"It was the people who needed to make this place work," Robert continued. "They needed you to be a charge."

"Your team will need to work with Kathy and Doc," Emily said as she steadied herself. "They have been working on trying to find a cure for years and have had mild success."

"Really?!" Robert said with surprise. "What do you call mild success?"

"They have a cure that can stop the effects of the bite depending on how long the bite has been on the person," Emily explained.

"All by studying the dead?" Robert said, deep in thought.

"No," Emily said, shaking her head. "All by studying and using my blood."

"A direct transfusion from someone immune to both air and bite transmission," Robert said with surprise.

“I’ve only done a direct transfusion once,” Emily said, glancing at Shawn. “We had the same blood type, and he lost a lot of blood.”

“I see,” Robert nodded. “I would be most interested to see their work.”

“We will need you guys to continue to wait in the quarantine cabin a bit longer,” Emily explained. “No one can come into Sanctuary until examined by Doc for bites. He’s been busy with everything that happened last night.”

“Of course,” Robert nodded as he went back through the door.

Emily felt Shawn’s arms wrap around her as soon as they were alone. She didn’t say anything as she felt herself melt into his embrace. The past twenty-four hours had pushed her past her breaking point, and she needed this. Shawn pulled her closer, and she felt herself beginning to relax. The weight on her shoulders seemed to slowly melt away.

“We still have a lot to do,” Shawn said after several minutes.

“I know,” Emily sighed as he let go of her.

Emily looked towards the gate and saw that Will was standing there.

“We’re ready,” Will said softly.

Emily knew he meant the funerals. Shawn took her hand and walked her toward the gate.

“Margaret says the kids are still sleeping,” Will said as they walked. “She’s going to stay with them so they can rest.”

Emily nodded as they neared where everyone had gathered. She watched as each casket was lifted and began its walk to the cemetery. They had spent too much time there over the past few weeks, and she hated it. Everyone stood quietly as Father Nathan spoke for the dead, and the caskets were lowered to the ground.

Everyone stood still, and Emily knew they were waiting for her to speak. Emily walked over to the grave she had made for Robert. Without a word, she kicked at the marker until it fell over. She could feel everyone's eyes on her, confused by her actions. When she finished, she turned back toward all of them.

"We have one more person to put to rest today," Emily said to them. "I made this grave years ago and believed I had laid to rest Robert Devow, the man who built Sanctuary. Today I learned this man was Trevor, Robert's assistant."

She could see the confusion on everyone's faces as she spoke.

"Trevor took his own life when things went bad, and Robert left his journals with Trevor," Emily continued. "He wanted people to believe that Trevor was him, so The General would stop looking for him."

"How do you know this?" Howard asked, stepping forward.

"One of the scientists we found," Emily replied. "He has only been with The General briefly,10. but was part of the original group tricked into making the virus."

"That doesn't make sense," Howard said. "There were only five, Sylvia died, and Robert...."

"Faked his death," Emily finished. "He hid outside the wall for years until The General found him."

Emily decided not to tell them about Robert telling The General about the emergency doors. She knew this information could break Howard, as June's death was still too fresh for him.

"He says he wants to work on finding the cure, to put the world back to how it was," Emily continued.

"Can he?" Julia asked.

"I don't know," Emily said, shaking her head. "But I think we owe it to those we have buried here to try."

Everyone nodded in agreement.

"So, he's taking back Sanctuary?" Cole asked.

Emily could hear the hint of aggravation in his voice as he spoke.

"No," Emily assured him. "He is requesting to join us."

Everyone stood, staring at her in silence. Emily shifted on her feet, feeling nervous.

"We have to try," Alec said, glancing at his wife's grave.

"I agree," Howard nodded after a moment.

Emily watched as everyone nodded in agreement with them.

"We will bring them in like anyone else," Emily said. "I just want to ensure we are all okay with it."

"We trust you," Julia smiled. "You've gotten us this far."

Emily felt herself blush with the compliment. The pressure of being in charge was more than she could bear most of the time, but knowing that they all trusted her gave her the strength to push on.

Emily waited as everyone said their final goodbyes to the dead and followed them back to the gate.

"I'll start on the exams," Doc said as she neared him.

"You're exhausted," Emily replied.

Doc's hair was messy, his clothes were wrinkled, and there were large bags under his eyes.

"You should go and get some rest," Emily said.

"I will," Doc assured her. "Once everyone is taken care of."

With that, Doc turned and headed for the quarantine area. Emily knew not to stop him, and she was too tired to try. Emily waited for him as he examined each scientist and said they were all cleared.

"Follow me," Emily said to them as Doc headed back to the clinic.

Emily had just led them through the gate when Hope ran at her.

"I'm late," Hope said with panic as she looked at the scientists.

"Right on time," Emily assured her.

She walked with Hope while she gave them the tour and the breakdown of the basic rules. Emily saw a smile spread across Robert's face as Hope told them that Robert had built Sanctuary. Hope ended her tour in front of the store as usual.

"Jessica will get you some clean clothes, and my mommy will help you through the rest of the process," Hope smiled at them. "I hope you want to join our family."

"You mean town," Gregory said with confusion.

"No," Hope said with a smile. "We're a family in here. Everyone looks after each other. We celebrate together and cry together."

"Who wouldn't want to join that?" Robert smiled.

"No one yet," Hope grinned back. "I'll see you all at dinner."

With that, Hope ran off towards the bakery. Emily knew that the other kids were there, all probably eating their late breakfast.

"She's an amazing girl," Robert smiled at Emily.

"She's the one I was pregnant with when I first arrived," Emily told him.

"Accelerated growth?" Robert said, looking back towards where Hope had run.

"Doc thinks it was due to the bite and the virus," Emily explained. "She seems to have slowed down for now."

"Interesting," Robert said, looking back at Emily.

Emily waited while they all went inside, and Jessica set them each up with fresh outfits. She walked them into her house and directed them to the showers.

"You've made it your own," Robert said, looking around. "It didn't have this much life when I was last here."

Emily looked around at the pictures on the wall, the toys stacked in a corner, the children's books on the shelf, and even the dog bed beside the couch.

"Can you excuse me?" Emily asked, turning towards the front door.

"Of course," Robert said, confused.

Emily walked out the door and headed straight to the clinic.

"Room two," Doc said as she walked in.

Emily walked straight to the room and opened the door. The lights were dim, but she could still make out the figure lying on the bed.

Emily walked over and carefully lay down, wrapping her arm over Marley.

"I'm here," Emily whispered to him.

Marley twitched slightly at her words. Emily carefully looked at his leg, which was now much shorter and bandaged.

"I'm here, baby boy," Emily cried as she ran her hand through his soft fur.

Chapter 19

The next day, Emily got the scientists settled into the apartments, and clean-up continued around Sanctuary. Jose was replacing the doors in the town hall, and people were trying their best to clean up the blood. She couldn't help with that today, though. She had something she had to do.

"Just in time," Doc smiled at her as she walked in. "He should be awake any moment."

Emily went straight to the room and sat on the bed. Marley appeared to still be under sedation, but Doc had pulled him off the meds hours ago. Emily barely saw him open his eyes, only to close them once again.

"I sure wish you would wake up soon," Emily said as she petted his head. "I miss you, boy."

Just as she thought, his tail began to give him away. The soft thumping sound on the bedspread brought a smile to Emily's face.

"It's been you and me from the start," Emily smiled. "And there's still a lot left to do."

Marley's tail continued to wag, but his eyes remained shut.

"I guess I'll come back later and check on you," Emily said as she moved to stand up.

Marley's eyes immediately shot open, and he began to lick at her.

"There you are," Emily laughed as she

petted him.

Marley attempted to stand on the bed out of excitement, only to learn he could not. He looked down to where his leg had been and let out a small whimper.

"It's okay," Emily assured him. "You are still the best-looking dog I've ever seen."

Marley looked up at her with his big brown eyes. She hated the sadness and defeat she saw in them.

"Let's get you up," Emily smiled at him.

As if on cue, Shawn walked into the room.

"He's awake," Shawn smiled at them.

"How's Dillon?" Emily asked.

She had visited Dillon a few times, but he was always asleep.

"Awake and talking non-stop," Shawn laughed. "Doc told me that Marley would need some help getting down.

Emily waited as Shawn walked over to the bed and carefully lifted Marley. He set Marley on the floor, holding him until he found his balance. Marley looked at Emily with worried eyes and didn't move.

"We've got you," Emily assured him as they kneeled.

Marley seemed to think about how to walk closer to her. He hopped forward on his front leg every several moments and began to walk toward her.

"There you go," Emily smiled as he reached her. "I knew you would figure it out."

Marley wagged his tail with excitement as he twisted his head to look at Shawn.

"Stairs and stuff will be a challenge for a while," Shawn smiled. "But I'll carry ya."

Emily and Shawn worked with Marley for a while as his confidence grew with his new way of walking. He learned quickly, and soon it looked natural to him.

"You want to go outside?" Emily asked him as she stood up.

Marley began to wag his tail faster as he walked towards the door. Emily smiled as she opened the door and followed Marley out.

"He's a strong one," Doc smiled as he saw Marley. "Remember, he may get tired more easily until he adjusts."

"How come everyone is always getting prescribed naps?" Shawn said, looking at Doc.

"Because no one here would rest otherwise," Doc laughed.

Emily followed Marley and opened the front door. Marley made his way outside but stopped.

"You getting tired?" Emily asked as she kneeled beside him.

Marley kept looking from one side of the street to the other. Emily looked up and could see why he was taken aback. The sight of the main street was still sickening. Though mostly dried, there were still clearly visible puddles of blood. Several windows were broken, and everything was stained in rust-brown blood. "I know," Emily said as she petted Marley. "I wish there was some way to wash it all away."

At that moment, Emily felt a raindrop hit the tip of her nose. She turned her gaze toward the sky but could not see a cloud anywhere. The raindrops began to fall around them, increasing in number. Emily watched as the water turned red and ran through the street. Marley took off running into the rain.

"Where are you going?" Emily called as she ran after him.

Marley's tail was wagging as he splashed his way around. Emily couldn't help but laugh as everyone began to join them. Hope walked towards her with a smile on her face.

"It's all being washed away," Hope grinned.

"It is," Emily nodded as the water ran down her face.

The day was cool, and the cold water made her shiver slightly. Her clothes began to cling to her skin as they were soaked in water.

"You remember that day we played in the rain?" Hope asked beside her.

Emily nodded yes with a smile.

"That was a good day," Hope smiled. "I wish we could have days like that again."

Emily glanced behind Hope and saw Shawn sneaking up behind her.

"Why can't we?" Emily asked Hope just as Shawn was nearing her.

Shawn moved quickly as he tagged Hope, and he and Emily took off running.

"Hey!" Hope yelled as she took off running after them.

It didn't take long for everyone to join them. They all forgot about the war that had stained the town. For an hour, they just played in the rain, letting the memory of that night be washed away around them. Marley was exhausted by the time the game was over, as the rain stopped.

"I should get him home," Emily said, looking at Marley, panting.

"You go on," Shawn smiled at her.

"The kids should get into some dry clothes," Emily said, looking at him with disapproval.

"Yes, ma'am," Shawn said, rolling his eyes.

Emily kissed him quickly and walked slowly with Marley back to the house. It took Marley a little while to figure out the stairs, but they were soon inside. Emily quickly grabbed a towel and dried off Marley's fur. Once she finished, Marley went to his bed and lay down. Within minutes, he was snoring.

Emily made her way upstairs and turned on the shower. She heard the others climb the stairs as she stepped under the warm water. She quickly showered and walked out of the bathroom with a towel.

"Damn," Shawn said, looking at her.

Emily blushed as she walked to the closet and got a fresh set of clothes. Shawn sat on the edge of the bed, never taking his eyes off her.

"Stop it," Emily laughed as she hurried back to the bathroom.

Shawn moved quickly as he stood and stopped the door from closing.

"Why?" he asked with a devilish smile.

"I…." Emily began, unsure of what to say.

"Am I not allowed to think my wife is beautiful?" Shawn asked as he pushed the door open, stepping closer to her.

Emily felt the blush in her cheeks deepen.

"I need to get dressed," Emily finally managed to say.

"Then just a kiss," Shawn said as he wrapped his arm around her waist and pulled her close.

"Just a kiss," Emily smiled back at him.

Shawn leaned down and pulled her deep into a kiss. Everything melted away as soon as their lips touched. Emily couldn't help but feel sad at the loss of contact when he pulled away.

"Get dressed," Shawn smiled as he stepped out and closed the door.

Emily stood in shock for a moment before quickly changing into her clothes. When she walked out of the bathroom, Shawn was gone. She looked around the house and saw that she was alone with Marley. Shawn and the kids must have quickly changed and headed back out. Marley was still lying on his bed, fast asleep.

Emily made her way through the living room, careful not to wake him up. Emily quietly closed the door behind herself as she left. Looking out at the street, she couldn't help but smile. There were tables and chairs set up. Shawn was helping to hang the lights around their party area.

"What's this?" Emily asked as she walked toward him.

"We had a vote," Shawn smiled. "We have been mourning for too long. Everyone wants to celebrate."

"What are we celebrating?" Emily asked, looking around.

While the rain had washed away most of the blood, there was still a lot of work to do.

"That we're still here," Shawn answered.

"Not all of us," Emily said, trying not to choke on the words as they came out.

"Don't do that," Shawn said, pulling close. "None of us would be here if it weren't for you."

Emily looked around as everyone started to join them. She knew deep down that he was right, but all she could think about was the people that they had lost. Everyone stood in silence, looking at her. Emily scanned the crowd and stopped when her eyes met Robert's. She still hadn't told everyone who he was. Emily slowly pulled away from Shawn. He put his arm around her and turned to face them all.

"We've all been through a lot," Emily said to them. "We have lost loved ones and managed to survive."

Everyone nodded in agreement. Emily looked at Alec as he pulled his children close to him. She looked over at Howard as he smiled at her slightly.

"I have recently learned something that all of you should know," Emily said, turning her gaze back to Robert. "You all know that Sanctuary was designed by Robert Devow. If it wasn't for him, none of us would be here. These walls keep us safe from what is outside."

Emily saw that everyone nodded once more.

"We've all seen his grave recently," Emily continued. "I have recently learned that it is not Robert that I laid to rest there but his assistant, Trevor."

Everyone looked at each other, confused.

"Robert set it up to look like he was dead to protect himself from The General, to keep working on a cure," Emily explained. "Little did The General know, Robert was trapped in his camp."

Everyone's gaze turned to the scientists who were standing in a group.

"I would like to introduce you all to Robert Devow," Emily said with a smile as she motioned for Robert to step forward.

Robert slowly walked towards her. He looked almost afraid that everyone would take the news of who he was badly.

"He has asked to live among us and continue his work," Emily said as he joined her. "I have decided to welcome him to join us."

"It would be an honor," Robert smiled at her.

"Now we really need to celebrate," Cole smiled.

Everyone began to clap, and within minutes, the music was turned on. The cool air gathered around them as they started the celebration. Cole handed out glasses of moonshine while the kids devoured the dessert table that Julia had set up.

Emily worked her way through the crowd with Shawn. Everyone wanted to talk to her, and she received more hugs and thanks than she could count. Shawn sensed she was growing tired and pulled her just outside the party.

"You all right?" Shawn asked her once they were alone.

"I'm fine," Emily said with a tight smile.

"You know you can't lie to me," Shawn said, looking at her sternly.

"It's just a lot to process," Emily sighed. "We've been fighting for so long. It's hard to believe it's over."

"I get that," Shawn nodded. "But it's over."

"I know," Emily sighed. "I just know there are other things out there that may try to attack us."

"And we'll handle it," Shawn said softly.

"There are still good people out there," Emily said, looking at the gate. "We have to help them."

"Then we will," Shawn assured her.

Emily looked back at him and could see the love in his eyes. She could barely believe how far her life had come in just a few short years. Shawn made her feel like a love-struck teenager whenever he looked at her.

"I love you," Emily said as she stepped closer to him.

"I love you too," Shawn smiled as he kissed her softly.

"Are you two going to hide over there all night?" Alec called them.

"Let's go," Shawn laughed as he took her hand and led her to the party.

They danced a few times. Emily pulled away from Shawn and found her way to the table, where she sat alone. She looked over at everyone. She knew each of their stories and smiled as she thought of everything that had changed in just a few short years, not only for them but for herself.

She had been in a loveless, abusive marriage. She found her strength and stood up for herself just before the world ended. She had waited to die after being bitten and not only lived but brought life into this world. She had faced and overcome more trials than she ever thought possible. Everyone here trusted her to keep them safe and ensure they got a chance to live. She had fallen in love with an amazing man and now had two young children who called her mom.

"Whatcha thinking about?" Joe asked as he sat down beside her.

"Everything," Emily smiled back at him.

"That's specific," Joe laughed.

"Just how far we've come," Emily laughed.

"You mean how far you've come," Joe corrected her. "It feels like we had that barbecue just yesterday."

"I never answered your question," Emily said, turning to him.

Joe looked at her, confused.

"She was a zombie," Emily smiled.

Joe let out a laugh, and Emily joined him.

"Thanks," Joe said as the laughter slowed.

"No problem," Emily grinned.

"Mind if I steal her?" Shawn asked, walking towards them.

"I should find Sarah," Joe said, standing up.

"Remember what I said!" Emily called after him as he left.

"I know!" Joe called back.

"What did you say?" Shawn asked as he offered her his hand.

"That if he hurt her, I'd throw him off the wall," Emily shrugged.

"Sounds about right," Shawn laughed.

"Where're the kids?" Emily asked, looking around.

"They wanted to stay tonight with your parents," Shawn smiled.

"Was it their idea or yours?" Emily asked, eyeing him.

"I may have suggested it," Shawn said with a shrug.

"Why would you do that?" Emily asked.

"You know why," Shawn grinned as he pulled her close.

"Maybe," Emily grinned.

Shawn quickly scooped her up and walked her bridal style back to the house. Emily smiled as she lay her head against him. She could still hear Marley snoring as the door opened. Shawn made his way through the living room and carried her upstairs. Shawn set her gently on the bed before turning and closing the bedroom door.

Chapter 20

The years passed quickly in Sanctuary. Sanctuary continued to grow with each passing year. Emily still knew the names of everyone inside the wall and treated them all like family.

Joe took his time, but after a few years, he finally proposed and married Sarah. The two started a family right away and soon had two daughters. Joe didn't like being the only man in the house, but loved the girls more than anything.

Rachael soon learned that raising teenagers inside the wall was no easier than it would have been before the flash. She and Emily became closer as they shared the struggles their kids were giving them as they grew.

Charlie and Christine enjoyed what they called their golden years. They were happy to have each of their children settled in a happy relationship. But their favorite part was being surrounded by their grandchildren.

Julia and Sam expanded their family with the birth of their daughter, Ashley. She was born a few years after the war. Bobby was protective of his younger sister. He remained the good-natured kid who had arrived with his parents many years ago.

Jacob met a girl named Bridgett a few years after the war. Unlike Joe, they moved quickly and were married within a year. They now had a son and continued living on the farm.

Cole remained single and focused his life on his daughters.

Alec never remarried. He focused on kids but kept the memory of his wife alive. He visited her grave frequently, leaving her flowers and talking to her for hours.

Dillon continued to settle into normal life. After a few years, he moved into an apartment and began dating Jacob's niece. It surprised them all. Jacob had been hesitant initially, but couldn't deny how good they were for each other. They moved slowly and eventually moved in together. While they were married, they had chosen to wait on the kids. Neither of them was sure if they wanted to have them or not.

Margaret outlived her husband for a few years, but did join him. It had nearly broken Emily the day she died. Margaret had become like a second mother to her. However, Margaret was ready to move on to the next life at ninetyseven.

Emily and Shawn continued to grow and love each other more every day. It took them years before they could even discuss having another child. After the miscarriage, Emily feared even trying again. Eventually, Shawn gave her the courage to do just that. They tried for a long time with no success. Doc had said she had scar tissue from the fall, and it would make it difficult, if not impossible, for her to get pregnant. They gave up focusing on it and decided that if it was meant to happen, it would.

Shawn had nearly exploded with excitement when Emily told him they were pregnant. She was worried her entire pregnancy, worried that something would happen. However, Lucy was born right on time and was perfect. They both agreed that their family was complete and decided not to have any more children.

Hope had officially entered her teenage years and was becoming more headstrong by the day. She wanted more than to live inside the wall and was constantly trying to find a way out. Steven was the opposite, content with the life he had. He had lived outside the wall before and had no desire to go back out unless he had to.

Life inside Sanctuary continued, and the people inside its walls didn't just survive but lived. Robert continued to work on the cure, but it was not their main focus. The main focus was life, to continue to grow and strengthen their family. There were still bad days, but they didn't focus on them. They worked daily to make a happy memory that could last a lifetime. For the time being, Emily and Sanctuary's adventures seemed to be over. Everyone was settled and living. However, the future still holds many unknowns....

Author's Note

Thank you for joining Emily and Marley on their journey. I hope you enjoyed their story as much as I did. If you could please review it, it would be greatly appreciated.

Are you looking for more? Please check out my other books.

Scan the QR code below for links to my social media, mailing list, and other books.

J.D. Crist

www.ingramcontent.com/pod-product-compliance
Lightning Source LLC
Chambersburg PA
CBHW011926300726
48970CB00008B/2593